BOOK FIVE

Double Trouble

Read all the Mackenzie Blue books:

MACKENZIE BLUE

MACKENZIE BLUE #2: THE SECRET CRUSH

MACKENZIE BLUE #3: FRIENDS FOREVER?

MACKENZIE BLUE #4: MIXED MESSAGES

MACKENZIE BLUE #5: DOUBLE TROUBLE

BOOK FIVE

Double Trouble

By

Tina Wells

Illustrations by Michael Segawa

HARPER

An Imprint of HarperCollinsPublishers

Conrad
Jen
Kathi
Missy
Marcus
Chloe

Mackenzie Blue and Her Crew

Double Trouble

 For information address HarperCollins Children's Books, a division of HarperCollins Publishers, 10 East 53rd Street, New York, NY 10022.
www.harpercollinschildrens.com

Library of Congress Cataloging-in-Publication Data

Wells, Tina.

Double trouble / by Tina Wells ; illustrations by Michael Segawa. — First edition.
pages cm. — (Mackenzie Blue ; book five)

Summary: "The continuing adventures of seventh-grader Mackenzie Blue as she juggles her time and attention between her auditions for a new TV pilot, preparing for the twins her mother is expecting, and working on a science project with her maybe-crush"— Provided by publisher.

ISBN 978-0-06-224412-3 (pbk.)

[1. Television programs—Fiction. 2. Auditions—Fiction. 3. Pregnancy—Fiction. 4. Science projects—Fiction. 5. Interpersonal relations—Fiction. 6. Friendship—Fiction. 7. Diaries—Fiction.] I. Segawa, Michael, illustrations. II. Title.

PZ7.W46846Dou 2014 2013032813
[Fic]—dc23 CIP
AC

Typography by Alison Klapthor

14 15 16 17 18 OPM 10 9 8 7 6 5 4 3 2 1

❖

First Edition

1

The Big Move

"Ummm . . . Zee?" Chloe Lawrence-Johnson raised an eyebrow as she held up an old sock with a googly eye and a Magic Marker mouth. She had found it while cleaning off the top of a bookcase in the bedroom of her best friend Mackenzie Blue Carmichael.

"Cool beans!" Zee said. "I was wondering where Mr. Sock Puppet was!"

"For how long?" Chloe asked. She stared at Zee from the top of the step stool she was standing on. "Five years?"

"Probably." Zee rushed over to take the puppet. She shook off the dust. "When I move into my new room, I'm going to make up for lost time and give him a place of honor where everyone can see him."

"Uh-huh," Chloe said skeptically. "Until he gets buried in an avalanche of clothes."

"No way! I'm turning over a new leaf," Zee said. "Now that I'm going to be a big sister to twins, I'm going to have to be way more responsible. Out with Zee the Messy, in with Zee the—"

"Well, it *is* true you're not going to be the baby of the family anymore," Chloe said, smiling. She glanced around Zee's room. Zee's school uniform lay on the floor, and her comforter was heaped in a pile in the middle of Zee's unmade bed. "But it's hard to change overnight."

Zee adjusted the bright-green bandanna that she had wrapped around her short red hair. "It doesn't need to be overnight. The twins aren't coming for a few weeks!"

"If you say so," Chloe said, picking up a headless Barbie that was jammed between the bookcase and the wall. "All of your books are boxed up. What do you want me to do now?"

Zee began to peel her Jonas Brothers poster from the wall. "Can you help me take this down?"

"Are you going to get rid of it?" Chloe reached up to loosen a corner. "It's autographed!"

"I've had this poster forever. It belongs in Old Zee's room."

"What will New Zee put up?"

Zee raised an eyebrow as she thought. "Maybe I'll get a Dakota Morning poster—since she's my favorite actor."

"Do you think you can get her to sign it, too?"

"*That* would be amazingly incredible!" Zee said. Once the poster was off the wall, Zee scanned the room. Her eyes fell on the closed closet door. "How about if we start packing up the closet together?"

As Zee flung open the doors, Chloe's mouth dropped open. Every shelf was piled high with clothes, games, and art supplies. "Zee! Don't you ever get rid of anything?"

"I've never had to," Zee answered with a shrug. "I've lived in this room my whole life." She grabbed a stuffed zebra from a shelf. "Besides, how do you throw away memories like Mr. Zebra?"

Chloe smiled. "I know what you mean. When we moved from Atlanta last summer, my parents made me give away a ton of stuff from my childhood."

"No way! Do you miss it?"

Chloe shrugged. "I thought I would. But now, not really."

"That's good." Zee took a box down from a shelf. "You can help me decide what to keep and what to throw away or donate."

"Knock, knock!" Ginny Carmichael, Zee's mother, called out as she stepped into Zee's room.

"We're in the closet!" Zee called to her mother, and then shouted, "I don't believe it!"

"What is it?" Mrs. Carmichael hurried over to the closet to find Zee clutching a tattered old blanket and a furless stuffed bunny.

Chloe pointed at the bunny. "Lemme guess. That's Mr. Rabbit."

“No,” Zee said, hugging the animal tighter. “Mr. Long Ears.”

“And your baby blanket!” Mrs. Carmichael said.

Chloe reached into a half-full box. “And here are your baby shoes!” she cried, pulling out a pair of small white leather boots.

“And my baby album,” Zee said, lifting an album stuffed with photos and paper out of the box. “Let’s look at it together!”

Sitting between her mother and Chloe on her bed, Zee began turning the pages and commenting on the photos. Some were taken before she was even born. In the first picture, Mrs. Carmichael was still pregnant. "I'd forgotten how enormous I was with you!" Zee's mother said with a laugh.

"Look at how long your hair was, Mom!" Zee exclaimed.

"Oh my gosh, Mrs. Carmichael! Is this your baby shower?" Chloe pointed to a picture of a pregnant Mrs. Carmichael sitting in a comfortable armchair, surrounded by women and a stack of presents. A giant pink cake with a white stork in the center sat on the low table in front of her.

"My best friends threw me showers for both Zee and Adam," Mrs. Carmichael explained. "That was before we moved to California. Do you remember visiting them in New York, Zee—Monica Flores and Joanne O'Neill?"

"Oh, yeah!" Zee said. "When I was about five, right?"

"That's right! Unfortunately, I haven't gotten to see them much since then, but we've stayed in touch."

"Are they going to throw you a shower again?" Chloe wondered.

Mrs. Carmichael looked at both Zee and Chloe and shook her head.

"It's not traditional to throw a shower for the third"—Zee's mother looked down at her large belly—"or fourth baby."

"But with twins, there's twice as much to celebrate!"

Chloe cried. "No offense, Zee."

"That doesn't offend me at all," Zee said. "Actually, that gives me an idea!"

"What?" Chloe and Mrs. Carmichael asked at the same time.

"We'll throw you a baby shower!"

"Oh, Zee, you've got so much going on already," Mrs. Carmichael said.

"Don't be crazy! The only things I have to worry about right now are school and The Beans," Zee said. "It's way doable!"

"Hey!" Chloe's high ponytail swung around her head. "The Beans could perform at the shower!"

"Cool! This is going to be the best baby shower ever!" Zee exclaimed. "It won't be a regular shower at all—it'll be a Baby Blast!"

"Can I help you plan it, Zee?" Chloe asked.

"Definitely! Let's go get some snacks and start coming up with our ideas."

The girls started to leave Zee's room when Mrs. Carmichael called, "I thought you were going to clean your closet!"

"I will. I promise!" Zee called back. "We just need to talk about a few ideas first—for the most fantabsome baby shower in the history of the world!"

* * *

"How about if we decide on a theme, then plan everything else around it?" Zee said, grabbing a handful of popcorn from a nearby bowl. She was stretched out on the couch in her family's TV room.

Chloe sat on the floor with her back against the sofa. "Awesome!" she agreed. "We just have to figure out what your mother likes."

"She likes to cook," Zee said.

"Yeah! It could be a cooking party!"

"Except I wouldn't want to make her cook at her shower."

"True. We should keep thinking."

Zee tried to focus, but her mind kept wandering. The day before, she and Chloe had performed with their band, The Beans, at Brookdale Day, a huge festival in town. The event also featured Bluetopia, the social networking site that their best friend Jasper Chapman had created. Kids all around the world had signed up for the site. But there was a glitch, and a lot of the users' secrets were revealed—including Zee's maybe-crush on Jasper. Zee and Chloe hadn't discussed the revelation all morning, and Zee really needed her best friend to help her sort it all out.

"This is so much fun, right?" Zee blurted out. "You and me. Me and you. Just us girls. Planning a shower."

"Uh-huh," Chloe said suspiciously, and turned her head to look at Zee.

"It's good for it to be just us—you know, without any guys—like Jasper."

"But we do things all the time without Jasper," Chloe reminded Zee. "He never comes to Wink with us when we get manicures."

"True. Guys and girls really are incredibly different."

Chloe shrugged. "I don't know. We also have a lot in common."

"I guess I'm just wondering if a girl can ever *really* be best friends with a guy. Ever wonder about that?"

Chloe stared at Zee without blinking. "Nuh-uh," she said matter-of-factly. "He's one of my best friends—just like you. It's not like with Marcus—or Landon."

Chloe had had a crush on Marcus Montgomery since she met him at the beginning of the year. And Zee had had one on Landon Beck since she could remember. They'd both started at Brookdale Academy in preschool. And lately it had been clear that he liked Zee, too. The only problem was, Zee didn't really feel that way about him anymore—which the Bluetopia blowup also revealed.

"But I'm sure Jasper would rather spend the day fixing Bluetopia than planning a shower," Chloe continued. "Although he's such a neat freak, he probably would have loved the chance to finally clean up your disgusting room."

"Hey!" Zee playfully knocked Chloe in the head with a sofa cushion. "It's not *that* bad," she said, then sheepishly added, "is it?"

Zee slipped the list inside her diary.

Baby Blast Themes

Western—Mom's afraid of horses (although I look cute in cowboy hats!)

Beach—Brookdale is right near the ocean, so that's not so exotic for us

Pajamas—This probably wouldn't be as much for Mom's friends as it would be for mine

Wacky hats—See "Pajamas"

Hi, Diary.

As you can see, that's the list of themes that Chloe and I came up with for the Baby Blast. And as you can also see, none of them work. Mom deserves something special—<u>really</u> special. (After all, she's the greatest mother in the world!) We'll keep thinking, but we better figure it out soon. Before you know it, those babies will be here. Which means . . .

Good News	Bad News
• I'm going to be a big sister very soon!	• I need to plan a shower—fast!
• I've got Chloe.	• Chloe didn't say one thing about everyone finding out that I MIGHT have a crush on Jasper. (OK, that has NOTHING to do with twins or planning a shower, but I didn't know how else to bring it up.)

Chloe, Jasper, and I are like peanut butter and jelly—and bread. We go together. So it would be really weird if I had a crush on him. Or would it? I mean, maybe Chloe didn't talk about it because she doesn't think it's such a big deal.

I used to think Landon was the cutest boy ever. I could barely think straight when he was around. But now I don't think I like him that way anymore. He's cute, but we don't seem to have anything to talk about. It's all pretty confusing and weird. Isn't it?

Zee

2

The Plan

Zee got down on her hands and knees and reached under her bed. "Gotcha!" she said, grabbing the Converse sneaker she had designed herself. It had a classic green inner top and a purple tie-dye pattern on the outer top. The outside folded down to reveal a purple lining.

Now where's the other one? she wondered, gazing around the room. Zee and Chloe had planned to get to school early to talk to Mr. Papademetriou, their first period instrumental music teacher, to ask if The Beans could play at the Baby Blast. But Zee had a lot of other stuff on her mind. She usually turned to her BFF Ally Stern when she was upset. Because Ally had known Zee since they were in preschool, she always had the best advice. But the Sterns had moved to France over the summer. It was a completely different time of day where Ally was! She wasn't even available to help on Skype. Zee decided to send her an email instead. Ally might not read it until later, but Zee knew it would help to write her thoughts down.

Bonjour!

Today is the first day I'll see Jasper and Landon since Bluetopia went ka-blue-y (LOL! Get it?). What am I going to say to them? "Hi, guys. Remember all that secret stuff that no one was ever supposed to know about? Just pretend you didn't find out about it."

OTOH, I would have been way too chicken to say anything to them myself, so it's kind of good they found out. Sort of. Mostly, it's just confusing.

Well, I have to finish getting ready for school now. Wish me luck!

Your freaking-out friend,

Zee

As Zee hit "Send" and watched the email disappear into cyberspace, she realized that she hadn't solved her problem yet. She still had to face the boys, and she had no idea what she would do. Mostly, she just wanted someone to talk to.

Just then, a text from Chloe appeared on Zee's phone:

>Don't 4get we r going to talk to Mr. P 2day.

Of course! Zee thought. *Chloe!* That's who she could talk to. Just because her conversation with Chloe hadn't gotten very far the day before didn't mean Chloe wouldn't have great advice if Zee just asked for it.

Zee typed quickly:

>Let's ride our bikes 2 school 2gether.

>Corner of Cranford and Chestnut?

>Sure! See you in 30 minutes.

Zee grabbed the other Converse sticking out from under her dresser and headed down to the kitchen for breakfast. Mr. and Mrs. Carmichael were already there with Zee's eighteen-year-old brother, Adam.

"You look bright-eyed and bushy-tailed," said J. P. Carmichael, Zee's father.

Zee grabbed a banana from the bowl of fruit in the middle of the breakfast table. "Chloe and I have to talk to Mr. P about the Baby Blast, so we need to get to school early," Zee explained.

Mr. Carmichael looked at the large clock on the kitchen wall. "We've got plenty of time, even if we have to leave a few minutes early," he told her. He often drove Zee to school since it was on his way to work.

"Ummm . . . well . . . Chloe's coming, too, so we're just

going to ride our bikes." Zee didn't want her dad to overhear her talking to Chloe about boys.

Mrs. Carmichael put a bowl of oatmeal at Zee's place at the table. "I'm sure Adam would be happy to drive you a little early and pick Chloe up on the w—"

"No!" Zee cut her off. "I mean, no, thanks," she added.

Adam looked at Zee curiously. "I smell seventh-grade girl drama."

"Drama? What drama? My friends don't have drama!"

Zee spoke so quickly, all of the words strung together into one.

"Oh, how about when Bluetopia exploded?" Adam teased.

Mrs. Carmichael flicked her hand in the air. "Oh, I'm sure everyone will forget all about that. The Beans made up and gave an *incredible* performance."

Adam stood up. "When it comes to Zee and her friends, back to *ab*normal is more like it."

Zee rolled her eyes. "I just don't know why I wouldn't want you to drive me to school," she said.

"Suit yourself," Adam said. "I'm not exactly heartbroken, although I would like to find out which 'cute boy' you're so desperate to talk about—as if I didn't already know."

Zee could feel the heat of embarrassment rise in her face. She felt like she was on fire.

"Are you sure you're OK riding your bike to school, Zee?" Mr. Carmichael asked.

"Of course. I'm fine," Zee said as she pulled her sneakers on and laced them up. "I'm just excited about seeing my friend, getting exercise, asking Mr. P about The Beans performing at the Baby Blast . . ." Zee stood up and headed toward the door that led to the garage, grabbing her backpack on the way.

“Bye, Zee!” Mrs. Carmichael called.

“Bye, Mom! Bye, Dad!” Zee yelled back. She heard her father’s phone ring as the door shut behind her.

Zee rode her bike down her driveway and toward the corner where she was going to meet Chloe. She still had a few minutes to plan what she was actually going to say to her friend.

“Hey, Chloe,” she said to herself, rehearsing her lines. “You know Jasper?”

No—that was no good. Of course Chloe knew Jasper.

She started over. “What do you think of Jasper?”

Ugh! That wouldn’t work either. Zee already knew Chloe thought Jasper was great. That’s why the three of them were best friends.

When Zee was about halfway to the corner, her phone sang with a text. *Not now!* Zee thought. She needed to meet Chloe soon. Still, she pulled her bike over to check the message—especially since it might be one of her parents.

When Zee looked at her phone, though, she saw that it was a message from Chloe. And when she read it, her stomach dropped to her feet.

>Jasper is at the corner with me. We can all ride 2gther.

Zee's stomach zoomed back up to her throat as she thought about seeing Jasper. *Calm down,* she told herself. *Obviously, what happened at Brookdale Day was not a big deal. Chloe doesn't think so, and Jasper probably doesn't think so, either.*

After all, Jasper was incredibly shy. If he really thought Zee *like* liked him, he probably wouldn't want to ride to school with her. Convinced that she was making a big deal out of nothing, she texted back:

>Great!

Zee pedaled faster to make up for lost time, sure that everything would be the same as it always had been. But as she got closer to the corner and her friends, she realized she was wrong.

3

Somebody That I Used to Know

From down the street on her bike, Zee could see Jasper squinting hard to bring her into focus. Jasper usually wore silver wire-rimmed glasses, but he wasn't wearing them. When Zee got closer, Jasper stopped squinting, and a smile spread across his face.

Jasper waved wildly. "Hi, Zee, isn't this a *rahther* funny coincidence that I'm riding my bike today, too?" he asked in his British accent.

"Yeah, pretty amazing," Zee mumbled.

"I've been telling Jasper all about the Baby Blast," Chloe put in.

Jasper nodded. "I'm sure Mr. P will agree that it's a brilliant idea for The Beans to perform at your mother's shower."

"What happened to your glasses?" Zee asked.

"I'm trying out contacts. I've had them for a while but I've never worn them before."

"Do they help you see better?"

"I suppose they take some getting used to," Jasper explained. "They keep moving around, which makes it hard to focus."

The missing glasses weren't the only thing that made typically neat Jasper look different. His white shirttail hung out of his uniform pants, his tie was loose around his neck, and a baseball cap was perched on top of his head. Although it was against Brookdale's dress code, some of the boys dressed that way and got away with it. One of those boys was Landon.

As they biked toward the school, Chloe and Jasper acted as though everything were perfectly normal. So Zee tried to do the same. Unfortunately, she wasn't very successful.

"So . . . um . . . what do you think the . . . um . . . you know . . . the band teacher—," Zee stammered. *Ohmylanta!*

Zee thought. Her head was spinning so much, she couldn't even remember his name!

"Mr. P?" Chloe asked.

"Yeah!" Zee said, relieved that Chloe came to her rescue. "I wonder what Mr. P is going to say about . . . uh . . . um . . ."

"The Beans playing at the Baby Blast?" Chloe said. "Did you get enough sleep last night, Zee?"

"Yes, Zee," Jasper agreed. "You don't seem quite yourself."

I *don't seem quite* my*self*? Zee screamed in her head. *You seem like a completely different person!*

"I'm fine," Zee said. *But I think I'll stop talking now.*

"Did you watch any soccer matches yesterday?" Chloe asked Jasper.

"After what happened at Brookdale Day, I mostly worked on reprogramming Bluetopia," Jasper said.

"Oh, how did it go?" Chloe asked.

"It's ready for everyone to start testing again," Jasper said. "Just The Beans and a few other people at first this time, though."

"That's awesome!" Chloe cheered. "Isn't it, Zee?"

Zee wasn't convinced. Now that all of Brookdale and Ally's friends in Europe knew Zee's secrets, she wasn't eager to "test" Jasper's site again. "Sure," she said halfheartedly.

"From now on, whenever I do any fixes, I'll be sure everything is running properly before I make the site live. Will you two help me test it?"

"Absolutely!" Chloe said.

"Brilliant!" Jasper said. "I've sent you and the rest of The Beans invitations. This time, *I* will be the only one who can invite people. That way, things won't go out of control." He paused. "I hope."

"Can't you watch soccer and work on the computer at the same time?" Chloe asked. "I try to watch the LA Galaxy whenever they're playing."

Zee didn't say anything. Since she wasn't an athlete like Chloe, or a huge fan like Jasper, she didn't always have much to add to their conversations about soccer.

"Chloe, I suspect we are boring Zee with our talk about football—I mean, soccer," Jasper said.

"Since when are you so worried about Zee being bored by soccer? We always talk about soccer."

Zee shrugged. "It's OK, Jasper. I'm sure you must get pretty bored by some of the stuff Chloe and I talk about."

"Like crafts, fashion, and manicures," Chloe put in.

"Not at all!" Jasper protested. "Actually, I find it all quite interesting."

"Really?" Chloe and Zee said together.

Jasper nodded in a way that didn't really convince Zee.

"It's no biggie," Zee assured him. "Music is the only thing we all really have totally in common. I guess it's something everyone shares. I mean, everyone likes *some* kind of music. It makes us happy. It makes us sad. It—"

Just as Zee realized she was rambling, the trio pulled up to the school grounds. Relieved, Zee rode up to the bike rack.

"Hi, Zee," someone called out behind her. Zee nearly ran right into the bike rack when she recognized Landon's voice. Slamming on the brakes, she stopped suddenly and turned around. Next to Landon stood his best friends, Marcus Montgomery and Conrad Mitori.

"*Awk*-ward," Conrad pretended to mumble.

"Really?" Marcus asked, looking around. "What's so awkward? I don't get it."

Chloe waved to Marcus and, once she parked her bike, walked over to him. Zee wasn't sure if she was walking toward him to explain what was awkward or to talk to him about something else. With Chloe going off, that left Zee with Landon and Jasper—and Conrad, who was having fun with Zee's embarrassment.

Landon pulled the huge backpack from his shoulders,

and it landed on the ground with a *thud*. For the first time, Zee noticed the books in Landon's arms.

Jasper noticed them, too. "What are those?" he asked.

"Books," Landon said. "For reading."

"Yes, I know what books are for," Jasper said. "I just didn't realize *you* did." Before Landon could respond, Jasper added, "You know, if you had a Kindle or Nook, you wouldn't have to carry so many books."

"Oh, I don't mind," Landon said. "I love books!"

"You *do*?" Zee asked. She had meant to say it in her head, but it accidentally popped out of her mouth.

Jasper laughed. "That's what I was going to say."

Landon nodded and looked right at Jasper. "Totally. And since I surf, I'm strong enough to handle a few heavy books."

"Hey, Jasper!" Conrad interrupted. "Looking good without the glasses."

"Why, thank you," Jasper said.

"But what's up with the untucked shirt and loose tie?" Conrad continued. "I thought that was Landon's thing."

Landon stood up a little straighter. Jasper pulled on the bottom of his shirt.

Zee looked from one boy to the other. Jasper was trying to be more like Landon, and Landon was trying to be more like Jasper!

Ohmylanta! Zee thought. It was as if Jasper thought that he could turn Zee's sort-of crush into a certain crush by being more like the boy she had been crushing on for years. And Landon thought he could make Zee like him again if he was more like the boy she was crushing on now!

As if all of that weren't bad enough, Kathi Barney and her best friend, Jen Calvarez, walked over to them.

Kathi stood right next to Zee. Zee didn't like to stand next to Kathi for lots of reasons. Kathi was really competitive and liked Landon, too—sometimes—so she was usually trying to embarrass Zee in front of him.

"Hi, guys!" Kathi said cheerfully.

Ugh! Zee thought, taking a deep breath. *Here it comes.* Behind her smile, Kathi always had an insult ready for Zee, Jasper, and Chloe. Even though Zee thought Jasper had gone overboard trying to change himself, she couldn't stand the thought of Kathi commenting on it.

"I was just on Bluetopia," Kathi said.

"Me too," Jen put in.

"And . . . ," Landon prompted them. From the eager look on his face, Zee thought that Landon expected the girls to say something obnoxious about what a disaster Bluetopia had been on Brookdale Day.

"Well, I just can't believe how quickly you fixed it,"

Kathi said, turning to Jasper.

Zee imagined what Kathi would say next. *Too bad you messed it up so badly the first time.*

Instead Kathi said, "I think it's better than ever."

Jen nodded. "You must be some kind of a genius."

"He's definitely a computer genius," Kathi agreed. "Maybe you can teach me some of that stuff sometime." Kathi was actually really smart, and amazing at anything she tried. She usually didn't ask for help from other people.

What's happening? Zee wondered, feeling as though she had stepped into an alternate universe. Then she remembered why she had come to school early in the first place.

Zee rushed over to Chloe, who was still talking to Marcus, and grabbed her arm. "Let's go!" Zee said, giving Chloe a little pull.

"But the bell hasn't rung yet," Chloe said, not moving.

"I know! But remember? We need to talk to Mr. P before it does!"

"I totally forgot!" Chloe said, starting to walk quickly toward the school.

With all the weirdness this morning, so had Zee.

4

Blast Off!

Chloe was telling Zee about Marcus's hilarious new joke as she and Zee headed toward their lockers.

"While you were goofing around with Marcus, I was stuck with Jasper and Landon," Zee told Chloe as she opened her locker and put some books on the top shelf. "They are acting *really* strange."

Chloe rolled her eyes and nodded. "That's why I hung out with Marcus."

"You noticed?" Zee asked, shocked.

"Well, obviously. I'd have to have my eyes taped shut not to notice, but I'm hoping if I ignore it, it will just go away."

"Maybe that's what I should do, too," Zee said.

"Is that really what you want?" Chloe asked her.

"I don't know."

"You could just find something else to think about," Chloe suggested, putting her arm in Zee's and starting to walk down the hall. "Let's go talk to Mr. P!"

Missy Vasi was already in the classroom when Zee and Chloe arrived. She stopped playing her violin and greeted them. "Hi! I was beginning to think I would be the only one here today."

"All of The Beans are here. They're just hanging outside talking," Chloe said.

"But you get to be the first to hear about our fantabsome idea!" Zee said. Then she turned to their teacher and said, "As long as Mr. P is OK with it."

Mr. P looked up from the paperwork on his desk. "What's up?"

"Well, you know how my mom is going to have a baby?" Zee began.

"Two babies!" Missy, who had twin brothers, put in enthusiastically.

Mr. P nodded. "Yes! Congratulations!"

"Well, I—I mean, Chloe

and I—had this idea to throw my mother an amazing baby shower."

"But it's going to be way better than a baby shower," Chloe added. "It's going to be a Baby Blast!"

Mr. P shook his head slightly. "It sounds great," he said, "but I'm not sure where *I* come in."

"I think it would make my mom really happy if The Beans could perform at the party."

"And it would be a great opportunity for the band, too," Chloe said.

"Yeah!" Missy cheered. "It would be so much fun to play a private party!"

Mr. P sighed, his shoulders slumping.

"What?" Zee asked. "Is it a horrible idea?"

"Not at all. That was a sigh of relief!" Mr. P told her. "The Beans don't have any gigs scheduled, so I was going to focus on fundamentals in class until we had one booked."

"Ugh!" Chloe said, her nose scrunching up.

"Exactly. I thought there was going to be a revolt," Mr. P told them. As the bell that marked the beginning of the school day rang overhead, the rest of The Beans walked into the room.

"Who's revolting?" Conrad asked.

"No one, I hope," Mr. P responded with a laugh.

"So we can do it?" Zee asked.

Mr. P nodded, his bangs flopping on his forehead.

"I can't wait!" Missy said. "Let me know if you need any help. I love planning this kind of stuff."

Zee could hardly believe what she saw next—Jasper and Kathi not only walked into class together, but Kathi was talking to Jasper. And although Jasper looked confused, he seemed to be listening to whatever Kathi was saying.

That's when Zee decided that she had not actually woken up that morning and was in the middle of a dream. She'd soon hear her alarm clock go off, wake up, have a completely normal bike ride to school, which would be followed by a completely normal day.

Zee waited. And waited. And waited some more.

"Would you like to tell the class what you told me?" a voice in Zee's dream asked.

There was a long a pause. Then Chloe elbowed Zee.

"Huh?" Zee asked, startled.

"Mr. P wants you to tell the class about the Baby Blast performance," Chloe whispered.

Zee looked around. All of the morning's weirdness was no dream at all. It was her life. "Ohmylanta," she mumbled before beginning to explain the Baby Blast. She told everyone about how she didn't want the twins' baby shower to be the usual baby shower and that one of the things that would make it really special would be if The Beans performed.

"The Beans? Perform at a baby shower?" Conrad asked.

"No way!" Marcus said, shaking his head furiously. "I am not going to be in the band at someone's *baby* shower."

"Are boys even allowed to go to baby showers?" Landon wondered aloud.

Zee had thought it was such a great idea, she had never even considered the fact that others might not agree.

"It's not going to be like a normal baby shower!" Chloe jumped in to save Zee. "This one is going to be *way* more awesome."

"Is it going to be a lot of moms sitting around and talking about how cute babies are?" Conrad asked.

"Probably," Zee said quietly.

"I'm out!" Marcus shouted.

"Why?" Jen asked. "I think it sounds like fun. I love babies."

"Exactly!" Marcus said. "Baby showers are for girls."

"But we can't play without all of The Beans," Missy said.

"I think you are going to have to," Conrad told her.

"I think it's a brilliant idea," Jasper said.

"Of course *you* would say that," Landon said.

Jasper glared at him. "What's that supposed to mean?"

Soon everyone had something to say—all at the same time.

Mr. P waved his hands in the air to quiet the class. "OK, everyone, quiet down. I'll give you a choice. We can use class time to prepare for Zee's Baby Blast—or we can go with my original plan of working on music fundamentals."

"You mean, like scales and stuff like that?" Conrad asked.

"That's exactly what I mean."

Marcus looked around the room. "Where do I sign up for the Baby Blast?"

5

The Big Break

Zee turned her phone on at the end of the school day. There was a text from her father:

>Waiting outside.

Zee hated for her father to pick her up in his SUV. Brookdale Academy was a LEED school, which meant they tried to do everything in an environmentally friendly way. In the mornings, she usually convinced him to drop her off a block away from the school. But as she walked out Brookdale's front doors, she immediately spotted her dad at the front of the car line.

Zee grabbed her bike from the bike rack and pushed it

over to where her father was waiting.

"Why aren't you at work?" Zee asked. Mr. Carmichael was editorial director for *Gala* magazine and usually wasn't home until later.

"I wanted to pick you up from school," Mr. Carmichael said.

"For no reason?"

Mr. Carmichael smiled. "Of course I have a reason."

"What is it?" Zee was having a hard time reading her father's expression.

"Get in and I'll tell you."

"But I rode my bike to school today, remember?" Zee pointed at her bike.

Mr. Carmichael jumped out of his SUV and went around to open the back door. "I'll load it in here. You can climb in the front."

As Mr. Carmichael pulled away from the school with Zee and her bike inside, Zee turned to her father. "This morning you didn't say anything about picking me up," she began. "What happened between then and now?" Then a rush of panic crashed over her like a wave. "Oh my gosh! Is everything OK with Mom and—?"

"Yes, yes, Zee! Your mom and the twins are fine," Mr. Carmichael interrupted her before she could finish.

"Adam?" Zee asked.

"Your brother is fine, too. I didn't mean to scare you. I didn't realize getting you from school would be such a big deal. I guess I should tell you what's going on before you jump to a crazy conclusion."

Zee waited anxiously but silently as her father turned at a traffic light. "I got a phone call from a TV show talent scout," he finally said. "He saw The Beans at Brookdale Day and really liked your performance."

Zee finally spoke. "He did?"

"And he wants you to audition for a TV pilot about a girl who sings in a local band and wants to be a rock star."

"That's like . . . the story of my life! I don't believe it!" Zee exclaimed.

Mr. Carmichael laughed. "I told him that ever since you were little, that's practically all you've ever talked about. They want an actor who can actually sing and play the guitar, too. He thought you'd be perfect—but of course you'll still have to audition."

"Will there be a lot of auditions?"

"The talent scout said that there would be—on-camera, off-camera, with other actors. I'm not quite sure how many. But don't worry. Your mother and I will get you some good coaches to help you get ready."

Suddenly, Zee stopped smiling and looked at her father.

"What's wrong?" her father asked.

"I think that you should tell the scout I can't do it," Zee said.

Mr. Carmichael looked confused. "Why? I thought you were excited about this."

"I am, but with the twins coming so soon, Mom has way too much going on to take me to lessons and auditions all the time."

"Hey! I can take you everywhere you need to be."

"But don't you have to be at your offices—or at meetings or photo shoots for the magazine?"

"I've got a great staff that can do all of that." Mr. Carmichael pointed to the iPad that was resting on the console between them. "And I can be connected all the time. When I'm not driving, I'll be sitting in waiting rooms. I can work there."

Zee's eyes lit up. "This is going to be amazing. I can't wait to tell The Beans! We're all going to be famous! I would give you a huge hug right now if you weren't driving."

Mr. Carmichael pulled into the family's driveway, then turned to Zee. "Oh, Zee, I thought you knew. You're the only one who has been invited to try out. This opportunity is just for you, not The Beans."

Zee looked down. The Beans were her friends—could she leave them out like this? She felt as though she had just gone from the top of a roller coaster to that part on the hill when you feel as though everything inside of you is in the wrong place.

"But they're my friends," Zee told her father.

"And I bet your friends wouldn't want you to miss such an incredible opportunity," he pointed out. "They will be happy for you. This is the big break you've been waiting for!"

Zee thought about it, and decided that her father was probably right. But she still needed to talk to her best friend

Ally about it. Zee ran into the house, shouted a hello to her mother, and raced up the steps to her bedroom. She couldn't wait to Skype Ally to tell her everything that was happening in her life, even if it was super-late in Paris.

"You've got to be kidding me!" Ally said through the computer screen. "Jasper was wearing a baseball cap? Does he even *like* baseball?"

"Crazy, right?" Zee said. "What I don't get is, if he knows I might like *him*, why is he acting so different?"

"He's probably trying to figure out what would make you *definitely* like him."

"But I do definitely like him," Zee said. "He's one of my very best friends—and my *only* guy best friend."

Ally shrugged. "I dunno. Do you think it's possible for a girl and guy to like each other so much and not *like* like each other?"

"I guess that's what I'm trying to figure out," Zee said. "But I can't worry about that now. I have to get ready for my mom's Baby Blast."

"I can't believe I'm going to miss your mom's big day. I wish I could have stayed longer." Not long before, Ally had surprised Zee with a two-week visit. It had been great to have Ally in Brookdale again, but now it seemed like a million years ago.

"I know," Zee agreed. "But you'll be like an honorary big sister to the twins. You can Skype with them, too."

Ally laughed. "Just make sure they don't short-circuit the keyboard with their drool."

"The Baby Blast isn't even the most exciting news!" Zee barely took a breath as she told her best friend about the TV pilot—and auditioning by herself, without The Beans.

"No way!" Ally said. "That is so amazing! I can't wait until the show comes to France. I am going to tell *everyone* that I know you."

Zee put her hands up like a stop sign in front of the computer screen. "First, I have to *audition.* And before that happens, Dad says I need coaching—singing, dancing, acting. Plus, after a pilot, the TV executives have to decide if they even want more episodes. And what about leaving The Beans behind?"

"Zee," Ally said, "The Beans wouldn't want you to miss out on a chance to make your dreams come true. And if

the TV people don't give you the part, they are crazy. And if they don't want a bunch of shows with you in them, they are even crazier."

Zee smiled. Even though Ally was thousands of miles away, she was always there for her.

"I don't get it," Adam said at dinner that night. "Does the talent scout know what a klutz Zee is?"

Zee looked at her brother as he took a bite of the couscous salad Mrs. Carmichael had prepared. "Why would they need to know that?"

"I just don't want you tripping into a camera. That could be dangerous."

"You're worried about me?" Zee said, surprised.

"No, I'm worried about the camera."

Mrs. Carmichael waved her hand in front of her. "Oh, Adam. Quit teasing your sister. She is not clumsy."

Well . . . , Zee thought. She *did* have a tendency to be a little klutzy—especially when she was nervous. And she realized that she was getting really nervous every time she thought about auditioning for this part.

"How is your homework coming?" Mrs. Carmichael asked Zee. "Being able to audition depends on your keeping up with your schoolwork. That's your number one priority."

"I'm almost done," Zee said. "I just have a little bit of French left."

"I'm sure Zee won't have any trouble getting her work done during auditions," Mr. Carmichael said. "I'll be keeping everything else organized." He reached for his iPad and a calendar appeared on the screen. "I've got it all right here—appointments with voice teachers and diction coaches, and the best routes to each studio." He looked at Zee. "You'll be able to do your homework in the car."

Zee turned to her mother, who was usually the family organizer and planner. A slow smile spread across Mrs. Carmichael's face, and Zee could tell she was happy not to be the one to plan all of the family's commitments for a change.

"Would it be OK for me to go upstairs now?" Zee asked. "I want to put more Baby Blast ideas together."

"Oh?" Zee's mother perked up. "Do you need any help?"

"No, I'm fine," Zee assured her. "Chloe and I are taking care of everything. You don't have to lift a finger."

Mrs. Carmichael relaxed in her chair. "I could get used to doing nothing," she said.

Zee hurried to her room and began making a list in her diary.

Stuff for the Baby Blast:

1. The Beans!
2. funky, fun, homemade decorations
3. a chocolate fountain

Pleased with her three big ideas, Zee stopped writing. She wanted to finish her homework early to prove to her parents that she was serious about the TV show *and* school. She wasn't going to mess up this amazing opportunity. She logged on to the Brookdale Academy website for French homework, clicked on the audio button, and began to play the assignment, repeating each phrase.

By the time Zee finished, she realized it was late and she hadn't had a chance to tell anyone besides Ally her big news about the show.

Should I tell Chloe or Jasper first? Zee wondered. Then she realized the thought of telling Jasper at all suddenly felt a little weird. But it also felt weird to tell Chloe without telling Jasper. And the idea of talking to Landon kind of freaked her out. Plus, who should tell Kathi? She'd probably be angry that the talent scout had asked Zee to try out for the show instead of her.

"Ohmylanta!" Zee said, looking at the computer screen. The solution was right in front of her!

She'd tell everyone all at once—with a doodle on her Bluetopia page. Jasper had asked her to help test the site, and this would be a good way to do it. She began typing an update next to her current profile photo, a picture of Dakota Morning.

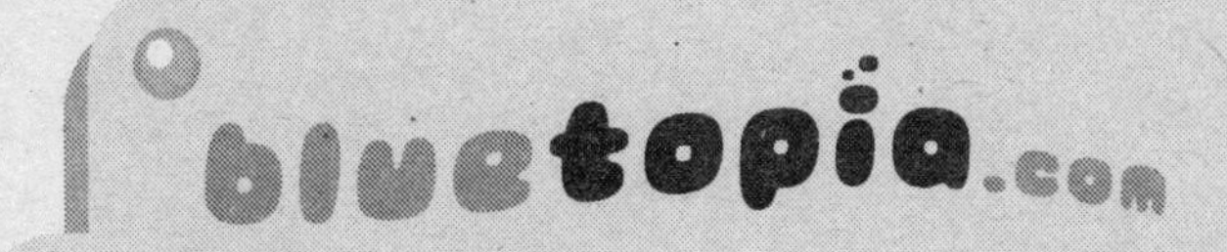

ONLINE
Username: Mackenzie Blue
Subject: Hey Beans!

Hey, Beans! I wanted everyone to hear my amazing news all at once. So here it is:

A talent scout wants me to try out for a TV show pilot. The show is about a girl who plays the guitar in a band!!!

I owe it all to you guys since the scout saw The Beans play at Brookdale Day. Pretty amazing, huh?

Thanks! You're the best bandmates anyone could have!

Zee read and reread the doodle. Then she took a deep breath, hit "Post," and went to bed.

How can it be?
Can it be true?
Here I am
looking at you.

6

Howdy, Partner!

As Zee walked across the Brookdale Academy campus the next day, she saw the rest of The Beans standing near the school's main entrance. Chloe waved when she saw Zee, but by the time Zee reached the group, everyone stood there silently.

"Hi," Zee said.

Everyone stared at her as if they expected her to say more, but Zee wondered what she was supposed to say. Maybe "Hey! Did everyone see my Bluetopia doodle?" or "Are you happy I've got the chance to do something amazingly cool?"

Luckily, Missy finally said something. "Congratulations on the TV show, Zee."

"Thanks!" Zee said. "It's not really a TV show yet. And I'm not in it yet, either. It's just an audition."

"Well, I think it's completely fab," Kathi said.

"You do?" Zee asked, surprised.

"Of course! Now I'll get to be The Beans' lead singer since you'll be so busy."

"I don't think I'm going to be *so* busy," Zee said.

"Are you kidding?" Kathi laughed. "TV actors have no life. It's constant work. And people who want to *be* TV actors have even less of a life."

Jen stepped forward. "So, if you're not going to be the lead singer, is there still going to be a Baby Blast—for *your* mother?"

"Definitely!" Zee responded. "I'm sure I'll still have

time for The Beans and the TV show."

"Why aren't we in the show, too?" Marcus asked.

"Yeah! We were at Brookdale Day, too," Conrad added.

Zee hadn't expected the question, so she wasn't ready with an answer. She could feel the mercury in her panic thermometer rising.

Chloe looked at the group. "Come on, Zee doesn't have any control over stuff like that."

"She could have refused to audition unless they included us," Landon said.

Zee turned to look at Landon. She was surprised to hear him join in with the others.

"Yeah! I've seen stuff like that happen on TV shows all the time," Jen added.

"I do not believe Zee could have reasonably refused a part she does not actually have yet," Jasper pointed out.

"Guys, this is crazy," Chloe said as she pulled Zee toward the school doors. Zee was relieved when Jasper followed behind them.

"Are you guys mad at me?" Zee whispered to Chloe and Jasper.

"No way!" Chloe said.

The threesome looked back at the rest of The Beans. "But I think they might be," Jasper said.

* * *

To Zee's relief, there was an all-school assembly during first period music class, when she usually practiced with The Beans. After that, Zee managed to make it through the first half of the day without any more confrontations. She just pretended to be intensely listening to the teachers, reading a book, or working hard on a math problem. Luckily, she also had most of her classes with either Chloe or Jasper, so she could talk to them whenever she was afraid to talk to any of the other Beans.

Lunch was more complicated—until Missy put her bagged lunch next to where Zee was sitting. "Sorry that I didn't speak up for you this morning," she said. "I think it's awesome that you were picked."

"You're not upset?" Zee asked.

Missy's shiny black hair swung across her back as she shook her head. "My dad works with Hollywood people all the time. I know how they can be." Mr. Vasi was a documentary filmmaker.

Zee rolled her eyes. "Yeah, my dad does, too."

"My dad says if you don't have any power, you can't change anyone's mind. So there's no way you can change their mind about including the rest of The Beans—until you are a famous celebrity."

"Can she make sure The Beans get on TV then?" Chloe wondered aloud.

"I don't know," Missy said. "But she'll probably be able to demand crazy things like special French bottled water to wash her hands and only red M&M's in her trailer."

"Or Froot Loops for every meal," Chloe added.

Zee put her finger on her chin and looked up as though she were deep in thought. "Hmmm," she said. "What *do* I want?"

The girls laughed. "Thanks, you guys. I feel so much better," Zee said. Then she turned to Chloe. "And I promise that I am still going to plan an incredible Baby Blast with you."

"Oh, I know," Chloe said, pulling a grilled tofu sandwich out of her lunch bag. "That's what best friends do."

"All right, everyone!" Ms. Merriweather called out as the bell marked the beginning of science class. "I've got a really important announcement to make, and I want to get started."

The students looked at one another as they headed for their seats at their lab tables.

Ms. Merriweather turned on the interactive whiteboard in front of the room. Without another word, she clicked on her laptop and began the presentation.

Pictures of laughing Brookdale Academy upper school students appeared on the screen. "Brookdale Academy is about discovery and exploration," the voiceover told the class. "And with state-of-the-art science labs, our students discover and explore in some of the best facilities."

Fast music began to play behind images of students wearing safety goggles and pouring liquids into beakers. "Students learn to think and experiment like scientists. They solve problems, answer questions, and show how the world works."

"We do?" Conrad shouted. When some students laughed, Ms. Merriweather put her finger over her lips to shush everyone.

On-screen, the camera zoomed out on a huge room full of science projects. Robots rolled across the floor, charts and diagrams covered walls, and plants lined counters. "The seventh grade science fair is coming. What will *you* teach the world?"

Everyone watched Ms. Merriweather anxiously as she began speaking to the class again. "Each seventh grader at Brookdale Academy is required to complete and present a science fair project. The school-wide winners will advance to regionals, the regional winners go to state, and the state winners go to nationals. For the past ten years, Brookdale Academy has had a winning project in the seventh grade

regional science fair. And we have had two state winners in that same time."

"Have we had any national winners?" Kathi asked.

"No, but there's always a first time," Ms. Merriweather said.

Kathi smiled, obviously thinking Ms. Merriweather was referring to her.

Everyone waited for what Ms. Merriweather would say next.

"You have some of the best science equipment at your disposal for your science fair projects. You may use anything you wish in the lab and do your work outside of the lab," Ms. Merriweather explained. "I will be here to help you with whatever you need. Ask me any questions you have during class, stop by after school, or email me if you'd like help with anything."

"I'd like help with the *whole* thing," Conrad joked.

"And if you want it, you'll get it," their teacher said.

Conrad looked shocked. "I will?"

"Yes, but not from me," Ms. Merriweather said. "Everyone may choose to work with a partner. You and your partner must contribute equally on the project. You will both participate in the presentation to the judges. And you will both receive a grade based on the judges' assessments. It will count as two test grades. This isn't a way to do less work, but rather to collaborate on a larger project."

Missy raised her hand. "Will you be one of the judges?"

"Great question," Ms. Merriweather said. "The judges will be local leaders in the scientific community. None of the Brookdale Academy staff will serve as judges. Are there any other questions?"

This time Jasper's hand shot in the air. "I think it's brilliant!" he said when Ms. Merriweather called on him.

"Thanks, Jasper!" The teacher waited, then looked sideways at him. "Do you have a question?"

"Uh . . . no . . . sorry," he said, blushing slightly. "Just that one . . . uh . . . comment."

Zee could understand why Jasper was so excited. The classroom science project he did with Chloe at the beginning of the year became a school-wide initiative. They came up with an idea to create vegetable gardens all around the school grounds. Now a lot of the food that was served in the cafeteria actually came from those gardens.

But Zee was not nearly as enthusiastic as Jasper. When she had decided to host the Baby Blast *and* audition for the TV show *and* keep up with all of her schoolwork, she hadn't expected to have a major science project on her plate.

Afraid of the answer, Zee asked, "Is it due soon?"

"It's due in six weeks," Ms. Merriweather said. "Now, for those of you who wish to work in pairs, why don't you go ahead and choose a partner?"

While the other students stood up and began moving around the room in search of partners, Zee sat still. She could feel her brain pushing against the sides of her skull.

Just as her head was about to explode from the pressure, she heard Jasper's voice. "Zee! Zee?"

Zee left her dream state and reentered reality, her head fully intact. "How long have you been talking to me?" she asked sheepishly.

"Just a second. I was asking if you want to be partners with Chloe and me."

Just as Jasper spoke, Chloe came back to the group. "Bad news, y'all. Ms. Merriweather says we can't have three in a group. It would disqualify us from regionals."

"Well, I certainly do not want to do that!" Jasper said in a way that sounded as though someone had just asked him to commit a crime.

Zee didn't know what to do. Clearly, Jasper and Chloe had decided to be partners when Zee was daydreaming. So they should be partners. On the other hand, with all that Zee needed to accomplish over the next six weeks, she *did* need a partner, preferably one who was good at science—which meant Jasper, Chloe, or Kathi. And there was no way it was going to be Kathi.

Zee looked from Jasper to Chloe, hoping the answer would jump out at her. It did—right out of Chloe's mouth. "You two should go ahead and be partners since Jasper and I were partners at the beginning of the year. I don't mind."

"Are you sure?" Zee asked. Sometimes it was really hard

having two best friends in your classes—and having a ton of work to get done.

Chloe nodded and Zee breathed a secret sigh of relief. Then the reality of what was ahead struck her. Zee had forgotten to think about how awkward it might be to be Jasper's science partner.

Or maybe it wouldn't be awkward at all, she thought. *We work together on stuff all the time. And that's not awkward. Usually.*

Zee felt a tap on her shoulder. When she turned around, Landon was standing there. "Yikes," Zee said, surprised.

"Huh?" Landon asked, pushing his blond bangs off his forehead.

"Oh, sorry," Zee said. "It's nothing. I mean—I was a little surprised. Even though you tapped my shoulder and I turned around and I should have expected someone to be there . . . I didn't. Expect someone to be there." Zee took a deep breath and wished for someone to hit the "Off" button. "That's all."

Landon ignored Zee's rambling. "I was just wondering if you want to be my science partner," he said.

Zee's mouth opened in surprise. "You're not still mad about this morning? About the TV show?"

"Nah. I was kind of mad at first, but it's not your fault people think you're amazing." Landon smiled.

"Uh . . . ," Zee stammered some more.

Chloe spoke up. "Zee is going to be Jasper's partner."

"Oh, OK," Landon said, turning to head back over to Marcus and Conrad—who were high-fiving each other as if they had just paired up.

"I'll be your partner if you want, though, Landon," Chloe said.

Landon turned back around and smiled. "Really? Awesome!"

Just then, Zee saw Kathi eye her, Jasper, Chloe, and

Landon from across the room and start walking over to them. Zee was certain that Kathi would ask Landon to be her partner. Now that Landon might have a crush on Zee, Kathi would be more interested than ever in working on a project with him.

But Kathi didn't stop, and moved right past Landon—to Jasper. "Do you want to be my partner?" she asked. "Chloe and Zee won't have to fight over you. And you'll be a lot more likely to get an A and go to regionals."

Now it was Jasper's turn to stammer. "Why . . . uh . . . I'm . . . uh . . ." He stared down at his feet.

"Jasper is going to be my partner, and Landon is going to be Chloe's," Zee explained.

Kathi looked at Zee, then turned on her heel so that her long brown hair rose up and down like a wave. "Whatev," she said, then she called out, "Hey, Jen! I changed my mind!"

Zee's eyes followed Kathi as she walked back toward her seat, and she noticed that

Missy was sitting in her usual spot at her lab table by herself, writing something in her notebook. Zee grabbed Chloe by the arm and pulled her in Missy's direction.

"What's up?" Zee asked Missy. "Did you get a partner?"

Before Zee could suggest another kid in the class to partner with, Missy shook her head and leaned closer. "I was *so* scared someone would ask me."

"You don't want to work with someone else?" Chloe asked.

"Not on this project," Missy said. "I started a science project at my other school and never got to finish it."

"What is it?" Zee asked.

"You won't tell anyone, will you?" Missy asked.

"Not hardly," Chloe said.

"Is it legal?" Zee asked.

"Definitely," Missy said. "It's just that it would ruin the test subjects if they knew what I am testing for."

"Test subjects?" Zee practically shouted.

"*Shhhh!*" Chloe and Missy said.

"Sorry!" Zee said.

Missy laughed and started whispering again. "That's OK. They're just psychological experiments. You know that my mom's a brain surgeon, right?" Zee and Chloe nodded. "Well, I thought it would be cool to do a project that really shows how the brain works."

"You're going to do that all by yourself?" Chloe asked.

"My mom has a lot of cool books, so she said she'd help me with figuring out my methods."

"Cool beans!" Zee said. But Zee was not feeling so cool. Putting together an awesome project was definitely going to take time. With everything going on in her life, Zee wasn't sure she had very much of it.

Zee and Jasper made plans to meet at the library after school to brainstorm ideas.

As usual, I was making a big deal out of nothing, Zee told herself when she remembered how worried she had been that things would be weird with Jasper. She was beginning to wonder if Jasper had even wanted to impress her when he wore his contacts and baseball cap the other day. Maybe he just felt like trying something different. He hadn't done it again.

I'm always trying out new styles and looks, Zee reminded herself. *Why shouldn't Jasper?*

When the dismissal bell rang at the end of the day, Zee hurried to her locker to grab her books. After she dropped them in her messenger bag, her phone buzzed with a text from her dad:

>I'm outside. We have an appointment with a photographer to get headshots to show an agent.

The door of Zee's locker closed with a soft *thud*. Then she headed down the main hall and out the school's front door. She needed to find Jasper right away so she could reschedule their brainstorming session for later. Luckily, as she stepped outside, she saw him—with Kathi.

Kathi was playing with her hair and laughing as Jasper talked. *Ohmylanta!* Zee silently groaned. *She's* flirting *with him!*

Was Jasper flirting back? Zee looked for clues that he was nervous. But Jasper wasn't looking awkwardly at the ground or pushing his glasses up onto his nose.

Phew! He wasn't as interested in Kathi as Kathi seemed to be in him all of a sudden.

But Zee wasn't sure what was really bothering her. Was she jealous? Or was she just sick of Kathi always trying to cause trouble?

"Hi," Zee said, breaking into their conversation.

"Oh, Zee," Kathi said, a hand on her hip. "We didn't see you there. It's kind of like you're invisible sometimes."

Zee decided to ignore Kathi. "My dad made an appointment for me," she explained to Jasper, pointing to where her dad was sitting in the pickup line. "I have to go with him, I think."

Jasper looked disappointed. "Oh, OK. We'll meet later."

"I promise I'll call you as soon as I'm done so we can figure out another time to brainstorm."

"It's not too late to switch partners!" Kathi loudly whispered to Jasper, as though Zee really wasn't there anymore.

Jasper stared at the ground and pushed his glasses up his nose.

Oh, no! Would Jasper really *rather* be Kathi's partner than be stuck with her? Zee would have to figure out a way to make up for bailing on him soon.

Zee walked toward her father's SUV. Even from so far away, she could see the wide smile on her dad's face. Which made her feel even worse. It was awful to feel as though she had to choose between her father and her best friend.

Zee climbed into Mr. Carmichael's SUV and smiled up at him. "Hey, Dad. Thanks for taking me to see the photographer."

This time, Zee had chosen her father. But she wondered for just one second if her dad liked his new role as stage father even more than she liked the idea of becoming a star one day.

Zee pulled out a notebook and began writing.

Hi, Diary.

The males in my life are making me crazy. Actually, only two males, but they are two of the most important ones. (And Adam is usually the male making me crazy, so that just shows you how amazingly mixed up everything is now.)

My dad keeps surprising me with appointments. He's acting like it's no big deal for me to change my plans. But it is. I have to think about my friends.

And Jasper now might like Kathi. What's so amazing about her? Except that she's kind of perfect. Perfect hair. Perfect teeth. Perfect face. And she'd probably be the perfect science partner for him. Unlike me.

"I'm really proud to see you so hard at work on your homework," Mr. Carmichael said, interrupting Zee's diary entry.

Zee looked up, startled. "What?" she asked. Then she closed the notebook. "Oh, yeah. I . . . uh . . . guess I'll finish this later."

"OK. I wanted to tell you a little bit about the photographer before you meet her, anyway. Veronica's done a dozen covers for *Gala*," Mr. Carmichael explained. "Three of them were our biggest sellers ever."

Zee couldn't help but feel herself growing more and more excited. "Are you serious?" Zee asked, amazed. "This is going to be so fantabsome!"

As Zee and her dad traveled down the freeway toward Los Angeles, any concerns about whether she really wanted to be a star—and whether her dad was going overboard—disappeared.

7

Say "Cheese"

Zee's hand shook a little as she pressed the elevator button for the twelfth floor, where the photographer's studio was.

"What are you so nervous about, Zee?" Mr. Carmichael asked.

Zee hid her hand behind her back. "I don't know," she answered. She looked into her reflection in the elevator door. "Maybe it's because my hair is doing some sticky-out-y and springy-doodle things."

"You'll be great," Zee's dad reassured her. "Remember, the photographer's job is to make you look your best—but also to help you look like yourself."

Zee smiled, then remembered she was still wearing her

school uniform. "Ohmylanta!" she cried, tugging on the bottom of the skirt. "I totally forgot I haven't changed!"

Before Mr. Carmichael could answer, the elevator suddenly *ding*ed, then stopped. The doors opened and, to Zee's amazement, Dakota Morning stepped inside. After the doors closed again, Zee wondered if it would be more embarrassing to faint or vomit. *Vomit would definitely be more embarrassing.* Unfortunately, that's exactly what she felt like doing.

Don't stare, don't stare, don't stare, Zee silently reminded herself. She reached up to the corner of her mouth and felt something wet. *Gross! Was that actual drool?* The best plan, Zee decided, was looking at her feet.

"I wish I had had style like yours when I was your age," Zee heard a female voice say.

Is that in my head—or in this elevator? Zee wondered.

"Then I wouldn't have minded wearing my uniform so

much," the voice continued.

Zee looked up. Dakota Morning was looking *right* at Zee! *The* Dakota Morning was actually *talking* to Zee!

Zee opened her mouth and tried her hardest to get some words out, but nothing would come.

"I think I wore the most hideous brown loafers ever known to humankind," Dakota said.

Zee couldn't believe that the girl standing in front of her in high black boots and a stylish cashmere sweaterdress had ever worn hideous brown anything—or a uniform.

"Thanks! At least this is better than what I had to wear last year," Zee finally managed to say. "The lower school uniform is a jumper."

"I'm sure you rocked it," Dakota said, winking at Zee. Then the elevator doors opened. "Oh, I think this is your floor."

"Uh-huh," Zee responded in a daze, her eyes fixed on Dakota.

Mr. Carmichael placed his hands on Zee's shoulders and gently guided her off the elevator. By the time she turned around to say good-bye, the doors had already closed.

"That was exciting!" Mr. Carmichael said, pointing down the hall. "We're this way."

Zee groaned. "If only. *Humiliating* was the word I was going to use."

Mr. Carmichael put his arm around Zee's shoulders and laughed. "*Or* you could just think about all of the nice compliments you just received and that a movie star likes your style."

Zee walked with her dad into a reception area and saw a younger girl with curly blond hair waiting with her mother. The mother was flipping through a large portfolio. Photos of her daughter covered the pages. Even from where Zee stood, she could see that the girl had appeared as a clothing model and in ads for amusement parks and restaurants.

Zee couldn't believe she was even allowed to be in the same room as a real professional.

"I was just wondering if you would sign my book." The younger girl held an autograph book out to Zee. Taylor Swift's, Daniel Radcliffe's, and Miranda Cosgrove's names leaped off the page.

Zee was sure the girl was confused. "Really? You want me to sign your autograph book?"

The little girl nodded so that her curls boinged a little. "I saw The Beans at Brookdale Day. I'm in lower school at Brookdale. You are my favorite band ever! And you're Mackenzie Blue Carmichael. I thought you were amazing!"

Whoa! Zee thought. Maybe Brookdale Day was more popular than she'd realized. With a huge smile, Zee scribbled her signature.

Mr. Carmichael grinned and spoke to the girl's mother. "Looks as though you have a real pro here!" he said.

The girl's mother studied Zee and her dad as if she was deciding how much time she actually wanted to invest in a conversation with them.

"Oh, yes. I've been taking Jenna Rae to auditions since she was a baby," the woman responded. "She's always been so beautiful and well-behaved that she's gotten a lot of modeling work."

"Oh?" Zee's father said. "Has she done any TV work?"

"Not yet. We've gone on a few auditions but we've never gotten a part."

We? Zee thought.

Jenna Rae's mother nodded her head in Zee's direction. "How about your daughter?"

"Well, we've been very lucky," Mr. Carmichael responded.

"You have?" the woman asked.

"We have?" Zee added.

"I mean, because we haven't had to audition. My daughter was discovered."

Jenna Rae's mother scanned Zee again and raised an eyebrow in a way that said, *"Discovered under what?"* But when she actually spoke, she said, "You certainly are lucky. Auditions are a full-time job. I'm sure we'll be seeing your daughter's name in lights one day soon."

"Oh, you will. It's Mackenzie Blue Carmichael," Zee's father said.

The woman's expression didn't change. "I know," she told him, then she looked away.

Zee was relieved when the receptionist put down her phone and said, "Jenna Rae, Ms. Chiang is ready. You can go right in."

"*Dad!* What was that about?" Zee asked, turning to her father, once Jenna Rae and her mom had left the reception area. Zee imagined Mr. Carmichael challenging every other young actress and her parents to a duel.

Mr. Carmichael jerked his head around to look at his daughter. "You noticed it, too? Talk about a stage parent!"

"No, I meant—"

"J. P.!" A woman with long black hair interrupted them as she rushed in their direction. She was wearing brown cowboy boots with a miniskirt and a leopard-print blouse over a black camisole.

"Veronica!" he said, standing, and giving the woman

a kiss on each cheek. "Thanks so much for doing this for me—and for Mackenzie." He gestured toward his daughter.

Zee smiled at the photographer. "It's so nice to meet you," she said, extending her hand. "Most people call me Zee."

"It's my pleasure!" Veronica said, shaking Zee's hand. "I love meeting new young actors." She leaned in closer to Zee and whispered, "They aren't as difficult as the big-name celebrities." Then she straightened up and started walking. "Come on. Let's go into the studio."

Zee followed close behind. "Thank you so much for doing my headshots. I know it was pretty last-minute."

"Well, when your dad told me what a huge deal this was and what a star you were going to be, how could I say no?"

The three of them entered a huge space with high ceilings and tall lights. Ladders leaned against the walls, and sunlight streamed through the floor-to-ceiling windows. Everything was white.

Veronica pointed to a high chair near a huge white backdrop that unrolled from the ceiling. "Why don't you take a

seat there, Zee, while I get a few things set up?"

"Isn't this exciting, Dad?" Zee turned to her father.

But Mr. Carmichael was looking down, his thumbs pounding out a message on his iPhone. He held up a single finger. "Sorry, Zee, I've got to get this one email out, or we could lose our April cover story."

There sure was a lot of waiting around in this business. With nothing else to do, Zee pulled out her notebook.

When you came along
I couldn't believe
That I'd fall in love.
I'm head over heels.
But now that you're here,
Whatever was true
Is now just a lie.
I was waiting for you.

"What are you working on?" Mr. Carmichael peered over at what Zee was writing.

Zee closed her notebook. "Just some song lyrics."

"Oh! For the auditions?"

"Probably," Zee said, shrugging.

"Well, I can't wait to hear what you come up with."

"Hi, Zee," one of Veronica's assistants interrupted the conversation. "I'm Nicole. I'm going to take you to makeup and wardrobe."

"Cool beans!" Zee said, sliding off her chair. Sometimes Zee's father brought makeup samples home from the magazine, and Zee wore them around the house. She had never worn makeup outside, though, because her parents wouldn't let her.

Zee followed Nicole to an area with a huge mirror surrounded by lights. "Tony will be doing your makeup," Nicole said.

Tony examined Zee's face and tucked some papers around her collar like a bib. Then he began applying foundation.

"Let's see what we can do about these freckles," he muttered with an intense look on his face.

Zee had always thought her freckles made her look at least two years younger than she really was, so if there was some way for Tony to make them go away, she'd be happy.

Tony scrunched up his mouth and grunted.

Zee giggled nervously. "I bet you've never seen this many freckles on one face."

Zee decided to let Tony work his magic and make the freckles disappear. She knew that after foundation would come eyeliner, eye shadow, blush, mascara, and lipstick. She thought about the makeovers she had seen in magazines and how different the "before" and "after" shots looked. She couldn't wait for her "after."

"So this is where you went!" Mr. Carmichael called to Zee as he approached the makeup area.

Zee stiffened, worried that once her father figured out what was going on, he'd shout, "Stop! Zee is too young to wear makeup. Take it all off!"

Instead he looked at Zee and said, "This is fun, isn't it?"

When the makeup artist was finished, Zee felt funny about the way she looked. She expected to love it. But she barely recognized the girl in the mirror. She felt like she was looking at a stranger.

After makeup, Nicole brought Zee to the styling area. Zee had never seen so many clothes in her life. Different sizes hung from racks. In the midst of pants, shirts, skirts, and dresses, Zee spotted a monkey suit and a Santa costume. Bookcases held clear containers of shoes, belts, scarves, and hats.

Nicole handed Zee a pile of clothes. "You can change into these behind the screen," she told her.

At last Zee could get out of her school uniform and into something normal! She put on the clothes and stepped from behind the screen.

Zee studied her reflection in a nearby mirror. She was wearing a color-block dress with fringe hanging off its layers of fabric and shiny multicolored leggings underneath. Short boots with high heels finished the look.

Ohmylanta! Zee thought. It was like nothing Zee ever wore. She wished she had had time to bring her own clothes—maybe even the gray wrap skirt she'd made. With a fun twist in the front, no one would ever suspect it was just a long piece of stretchy fabric. Or the short-sleeve T-shirt she'd cut leaf shapes out of. She wore it over a bright orange T-shirt so that the leaf cutouts were orange.

All of Zee's creations cost a teeny fraction of the price of what she had on—and looked way better on her.

Veronica rushed over. "You look amazing!" she said enthusiastically. "You are going to photograph so well in that."

"These clothes are really, really nice, but not exactly my style," Zee said carefully. "Can I try something more like what I usually wear?" she asked her father.

Veronica turned to Mr. Carmichael. She didn't say anything, but she looked anxious.

"The clothes you wear for professional photographs are different from what you wear with your friends," Zee's father explained. "Think about all of the celebrities who've appeared in *Gala*. They don't normally dress like they do in the magazine. We're creating a story—an image."

"I thought they were celebrities because people liked their image," Zee said. "I thought the talent scout liked *my* image."

Mr. Carmichael put a hand on each of Zee's shoulders. "They do, but acting is about becoming another character. If you want to be an actor, you'll need to get used to adopting new styles."

"I don't want to be an actor," Zee said. "I want to be a rock star."

Mr. Carmichael glanced at Veronica, and then said to Zee, "But the role in the TV show is to play a rock star—that's the first step."

"That's true," Zee agreed, without looking him in the eyes. Her stomach turned and knotted a little. Was it true? Or was Zee just agreeing because that's what her dad wanted her to do?

"This is really just for some headshots," Veronica said. "The clothes you're wearing won't even show in the photo. It's all about *you*."

Zee looked at her father. "For now, you just need to listen to the experts," Mr. Carmichael said. "When you're a famous musician, you'll get to call the shots."

Will I? Zee wasn't sure. Besides, she really didn't want to call the shots. She just wanted to be herself. And she thought that's what her father and the talent scout wanted, too.

8

Somebody That I Used to Know: The Sequel

Hola, Diary.

I just finished with my first big Hollywood experience—getting my headshots taken. Some really amazing stuff happened—like having a professional makeup artist put my makeup on and having people get me whatever I needed and do things for me. But some not-so-great stuff happened too—like when I basically turned into someone completely different.

Actually, the past couple of days have definitely been the weirdest ones of my life. But they've also been exciting. I can't figure out if they have been more weird or more exciting, though. So I need your help.

More Exciting	More Weird
1. I actually met Dakota Morning.	1. My father seems REALLY into my being on this show. What if I don't get it?
2. Everyone compliments me and says nice things to me.	2. I'm not really sure what my BFFs think (except for Ally ☺).
3. I get to see what happens behind the scenes. (So far it's a lot of waiting, which is a little boring, but I still think it belongs in this column.)	3. Some of my friends are not happy with me.
	4. Boys. Do I have to say more?

Uh-oh. There are more "More Weird" than "More Exciting" things. I already bailed on Jasper and the science fair project by going to the photo shoot. But once all of the big stuff is over with, I'm sure I'll have more time for school.

"We're home!" Mr. Carmichael announced as he pressed the button to open the garage door.

"Finally!" Zee said as she climbed out of her father's SUV. "I never knew having your picture taken could be so exhausting." After all, on school picture day, she just sat on a chair in front of a blank backdrop, smiled, and headed back to class. This photo shoot involved a lot of changing, redoing, re-redoing, and trying on more facial expressions than she realized one human being could make.

Mr. Carmichael *mmm-hmm*ed in agreement. "But it's fun, too, right?"

"Maybe you should ask me tomorrow," Zee said. "I can hardly even think straight right now."

Zee had just two things planned for the evening:

1. Eat dinner.

2. Do homework.

Actually, it was three things if you counted

3. Go to sleep.

At the moment, Zee definitely counted all three.

When Zee walked into the house with her father, she saw Chloe and Missy sitting in the TV room with her mother.

"Wowee!" Chloe exclaimed. "I hardly recognize you."

"I've never seen you wear makeup," Missy said.

Zee scrunched up her nose. "How bad do I look?"

"You don't look bad to me," Chloe explained. "You just don't look like yourself."

"Have you guys been waiting for me to come home?" Zee asked her friends. "I'm sorry it took so long."

"Actually, we were just helping your mom with the Baby Blast," Missy said. Then she added, "I hope it's OK that I'm helping, too."

Zee dropped her backpack on the ground, suddenly getting a new burst of energy. "Of course it is! I can't wait to hear what you've come up with."

"While the girls fill you in, Zee, I'll go heat up some dinner for you and Dad," Mrs. Carmichael said, extending her arm in front of her. "If you help me up, I might be able to waddle into the kitchen."

Zee grabbed her mother's hand and pulled her off the couch, then sat down between Chloe and Missy. "Tell me everything!"

"My mom told me about this game that everyone played at her baby shower," Chloe said. "Each guest brings a photo of herself as a baby. Then someone puts all of the photos on a board so everyone can guess who's who!"

"And the person who has the most correct answers wins a prize!" Missy finished.

"Hmm." Zee tried to sound enthusiastic, but she wanted

the Baby Blast activities to be more modern and not so old-fashioned. Still, she wasn't sure how to tell her friends. "Did you ask my mom if she wants that kind of game?"

"Yeah," Chloe said. "She said it sounded fun."

"Oh, OK," Zee said. "Then I guess it's OK."

"Do you want to hear about the party favors?" Missy asked.

"Yes! Definitely," Zee said.

"I thought it would be really cute to have baby bottles for each guest and put things related to the theme in each one. Like jelly beans that are the same color as the decorations."

Zee forced a smile.

"What's wrong?" Chloe asked.

"I don't know," Zee said. "I was just thinking the shower would be a little more . . . different than the usual baby shower."

"Like how?" Chloe asked.

"Why don't you tell us some of your ideas?" Missy suggested.

"Well, with everything that's been going on lately, I haven't really come up with anything *definite*."

"So, I guess you don't want to hear what other ideas we had?" Chloe asked.

Zee could hear the irritation growing in Chloe's voice. "I just wish you had waited for me to be here so that we could all plan the shower together," she explained.

Missy gave Chloe a sideways look.

"What's that supposed to mean?" Zee asked.

"Well . . . your mom is about to have the twins," Missy said. "And you've got your TV show and are really busy."

"And that's really awesome," Chloe put in.

"But you made a really good point that your mom deserves a really cool shower, and we want to help her—and you—out," Missy finished.

Zee stood up. "This shower is for *my* mother. It was my idea, and I should be the one planning it—*and* deciding who should help plan it."

Chloe and Missy popped out of their seats, too. "Not everything is about you, Zee!" Chloe said, walking toward the Carmichaels' front door.

"I never said it was!" Zee said, wishing she could take back what she'd said before.

Missy followed Chloe out of Zee's house. "No," she said quietly, "but you're kind of acting that way."

Zee watched the door close behind them, then spun around. Her mother was standing in front of her.

"What happened?" Mrs. Carmichael asked.

"I can't believe they went ahead and started planning the Baby Blast without me. And when I told them their ideas might not work, they got really mad."

"Maybe because they did work really hard on their ideas," Mrs. Carmichael said. "But we wished you were here with us the whole time."

"I know," Zee said, confused. She knew they just wanted to help out, and it was awesome her friends were excited about the twins. "But they were all just *their* ideas. The twins are going to be my siblings—not theirs."

"We know that, honey," Mrs. Carmichael said. "You and Adam will be the most important people in the twins' lives."

Zee crossed her arms. "At least I'll be one of the most important people in *somebody's* life," she muttered. She knew she was tired and overreacting. Still, she couldn't stop herself. Or maybe she just wanted her mother to reassure her. "It's like you don't even need me anymore—now that you have Chloe and Missy," she muttered.

Mrs. Carmichael gave Zee a hug. "Oh, Zee, I do too need you. So does your father. And there's still a lot to do to get ready for the shower. But the twins will be here soon. Let your friends help you."

Zee hung her head. "I just wanted the shower to be the best baby shower ever."

"With you and The Beans performing, it *will* be."

"That wasn't even my idea! It was Chloe's. I haven't done anything for the Baby Blast—or for you, Mom."

"But you'll be there to play with The Beans—and to celebrate with us. For now, just focus on the TV pilot and your schoolwork, and the rest will fall into place."

"OK," Zee said, feeling a little bit better about missing the Baby Blast planning. "But can I focus on dinner now? I'm *so* hungry!"

After dinner, Zee went up to her room to do homework. But first, she had to get her thoughts into her diary.

Hi, Diary.

I hope that this TV show doesn't ruin my friendships. I feel like things are already messed up—and I'm just getting started. It's so weird. I mean, I used to hang out with them all the time—during school, during practice, at Wink and our houses. Now I'm spending my time with Dad. Which is great, because he's great. But I thought I would be able to do it all. Mom's right, though. I can't. I have to figure out what I want to do most.

I just hope I'm making the right choice.

Zee

When Zee closed the last textbook, she breathed a sigh of relief.

"Done with homework!" she announced to herself. Now she could wash all of the makeup off her face and crawl into bed. It had been a long day, and all she could think about was how incredible it would be to finally get some sleep.

When Zee stood up, her phone buzzed with a text from Jasper.

>What are ur ideas for the science fair project?

Ohmylanta! Zee thought. *I can't believe I forgot about science! And Jasper!* Chloe and Missy were already mad at Zee—and Zee knew she had to apologize to her friends tomorrow. She didn't want Jasper to be mad at her, too.

Zee wondered how she was going to freeze time long enough to research science topics, type up all the information into notes, and send them to Jasper before tomorrow morning. She sent another text:

>I will send them to you before school tomorrow.

Now she didn't have to confess that she hadn't actually done any work. She just had to stay awake a little longer and come up with a few good ideas.

But before she could focus on the science fair, Zee wanted to talk to Ally. Ally was probably still asleep, but maybe getting some of her thoughts down in an email would help. Zee hoped she would wake up to some good advice from her best friend.

Zee brought the laptop to her bed and began typing.

Hey, Ally!
SO MUCH has happened incredibly fast. I feel like it's been a year since we Skyped!!
At first, I was kind of upset that my dad and the photographer who took my headshots today were making all of the decisions FOR me. Then I

thought about it and couldn't believe I was complaining. This is the greatest opportunity of my ENTIRE life. Plus, meeting Dakota Morning makes up for all of the bad stuff. That's right! I met Dakota Morning!!! She even talked to me!

Unfortunately, Chloe, Missy, and I had a fight. I think it was because I was just tired. (And kind of jealous that they have more time than I do to plan Mom's shower.)

Mom thinks I'm trying to do too much. But my life is going to be like this for a while. I hope my friends understand.

Including Jasper. He's my partner for the science fair project. I really don't want to upset Jasper by being a bad partner. With the auditions and getting ready for the auditions, I'm afraid I could be. I hope he'll understand.

You would. Wouldn't you?

LYLAS,

Yr BFF

Zee hit "Send," then began researching topics for the science fair project, but she wasn't sure where to begin. Still, she wanted to prove to Jasper that she could be a good science fair partner. All she needed to do was find the perfect project idea.

Zee clicked on the links and examined the images and explanations on the screen. *Too hard,* she said to herself as she rejected the first idea. *Too boring.* She made the next one disappear. One after another, she scrolled through project ideas.

Too young.

Too time-consuming.

Too blah.

Zee wasn't sure exactly how many she looked at, though, because she soon fell asleep, without taking any of the notes she had promised Jasper.

9

Ally's Advice

The next morning, Adam drove Zee to school in his little red car. She checked her emails on the way and was happy to see she had gotten a response from Ally.

> Hi, Zee.
> You met Dakota Morning?! Awesome! ☺ I would have fainted!
> Still, you must be feeling really horrible about your fight with Chloe and Missy. When I first moved to France, I hated that I was missing all the fun stuff happening in Brookdale. And I was a little jealous of Chloe and Jasper. (OK, maybe REALLY jealous.) Then I realized that even though I was

missing out, some cool things were happening in my life, too. (After all, I live in Paris!)
Plus, your mom is completely awesome, and of course, everyone wants to help her out. I wish I could be there to plan the party, too. ☺ (Another cool thing I'm missing.) It looks like you might not really have the time to plan it. So maybe you should tell Chloe and Missy your ideas but let them make the final decisions with Ginny.

Zee thought about her best friend's advice and realized that it made a lot of sense. Chloe and Missy were trying to help out because they were awesome friends. They hadn't been trying to hurt Zee. She kept reading.

Don't take this the wrong way, but be careful that you don't take advantage of Jasper. He's a really great friend and he would never leave YOU hanging. Besides, lots of study dates could be the perfect way to figure out if you really like him. ☺
Heart,
A

Zee knew Ally was right. She also knew that she had to

make up with Chloe and Missy as soon as possible and set things right. And she couldn't do it with a text or with an email. It had to be in person.

As soon as Adam parked in the student lot, Zee flung open the door and scanned the campus. None of her friends were in sight. In fact, hardly anyone was still outside.

The first bell had rung—and if Zee didn't hurry, she would miss the late bell, too. She rushed past the rows of solar panels that provided a lot of the electricity for Brookdale Academy, toward the main doors.

"Don't bother thanking me!" Adam called behind her.

"Thanks, Adam!" Zee yelled back.

The late bell rang just as Zee passed through the doorway to Mr. P's class. She took a seat near Chloe and Missy. They were turned away from her, so she couldn't even try to apologize to them now. But the fact that they were purposely ignoring her stung.

Zee glanced at where Jasper was sitting. By now, he had figured out that she hadn't sent him her notes for the science project. She was relieved that class was starting and she didn't have to explain herself to him.

"Everyone, get your instruments out," Mr. P called out, "and let's get started!"

As Zee snapped open her stars-and-stripes studded

guitar case, Landon waved and smiled at her from across the room. Zee waved back but tried not to smile too big. She didn't want him to think it was a crush-smile instead of a friend-smile. Not long before, just having Landon look in her direction would have made her happy for the rest of the day. Now it only made her feel worse, since she didn't like him like that anymore. Still, Landon was just about the only person being friendly to her.

Zee had noticed that Landon had seemed a little lonely in school lately. Kathi didn't fawn all over him like she used to. And Marcus and Conrad seemed like two halves of the same brain. They were always working as a team to crack everyone up—or protest something together. Their routine often didn't include Landon, who was Marcus's best friend until Conrad moved to Brookdale.

Zee could definitely relate to Landon, since she was feeling more alone than usual these days.

"When you're ready," Mr. P said again, "everyone can begin rehearsing the songs you'll be playing at Mrs. Carmichael's Baby Blast." Students began to move from their seats. "Except Zee. We'll work on your audition pieces together."

"Hey, Mr. P!" Marcus protested. "Why does Zee get special treatment?"

"Yeah," Conrad said. "There are way more of us than there are of her."

Zee spoke up. "It's fine, Mr. P. I can just work on my songs by myself at home. Besides, I should rehearse for the Baby Blast, too." But the fact of the matter was, Zee had not actually even thought about what songs she might perform for her audition, so she was relieved that Mr. P wanted to help her.

Mr. P put up his hands as if he were about to surrender. Then he said, "Don't worry. I've got this figured out." He pointed to Zee. "You were discovered at a Beans performance, which means you are representing The Beans at your audition. I just want to go over the songs you want to play to make sure they show off your musical strengths."

Mr. P looked around at the rest of the students. "Kathi will lead the Baby Blast rehearsals."

Kathi clapped her hands then rubbed them together as if she were a scientist who had just come up with an evil plan. "Does this mean I'm also the lead singer?" Kathi asked. "It's no prob if I am."

"Since Zee has her hands full with the TV show, I think that would be a good idea." Mr. P looked from Kathi to Zee. "That *would* be one less thing for you to have to worry about right now."

"I won't be part of the Baby Blast?" Zee asked.

"Of course you will," Mr. P responded.

"She will?" Kathi looked stunned.

"You just won't be performing," Mr. P told her. "Your dad and I decided that at this point it's probably not realistic."

Zee sank into her seat. In less than twenty-four hours, she had lost all control over the Baby Blast—first the planning, and now the music.

The worst part was that Kathi had been right yesterday. She was now the lead singer and Zee wasn't even a Bean anymore.

Actually, the worst part was that Zee's dad had talked to Mr. P about what was "realistic" or not—without asking her.

Kathi turned to The Beans. "OK, everyone. Let's figure out which songs will highlight my voice."

Zee glanced over at Chloe and Jasper, hoping to make eye contact so she could give them a sympathetic look. She knew what it was like to be bossed around by Kathi. Instead, neither one looked at Zee at all. They just took their places with the rest of the group so that rehearsal could begin. Missy avoided looking her way, too.

Mr. P and Zee found a corner of the room where it would be quiet enough for them to work. "I was thinking that for this audition, you probably want to pick a few different kinds of songs so you can show your range," Mr. P told her. "You could do a couple that you wrote and then a popular song that they'll recognize."

Zee's teacher continued to talk, and Zee tried to listen, but she kept getting distracted by The Beans rehearsal across the room. Kathi sounded amazing, and with everyone doing exactly what she told them to, so did The Beans. Every so often, Zee would hear Kathi squeal something like, "That's *such* a great idea, Jasper!" Whenever she did, Jasper's face would turn beet red as he grinned from ear to ear.

Kathi's behavior might have been tolerable if Chloe had looked over and made a face about it, but she didn't. Instead, everyone acted as if Zee wasn't even in the room.

"When you were in Yes No, did you and the other band members ever fight?" Zee asked Mr. P. She knew that his band had been pretty successful when they were together. They'd even toured Europe and made it onto the cover of *Gala*.

Mr. P looked at the other students, then leaned forward. "All the time."

"So you weren't friends?"

"They were my best friends," Mr. P said, looking surprised. "They still are."

"Then why did you fight all of the time?"

"I guess because we knew we would always make up because we really cared about one another. But it was also because we all just really cared about the music, and sometimes people who are passionate disagree about the best way to do the thing they're passionate about."

"So how did you figure out who to listen to?" Zee asked.

"You have to make sure everyone gets a turn being right. No one is right all of the time—or even most of the time. But everyone is right some of the time."

Zee let Mr. P's words sink in. "Maybe it's a good idea to figure out what it matters most to be right about."

"When you're in a band, sometimes you just have to let people do their own thing. Making a fair contribution is the most important part."

"It's true for science projects, too," Zee added.

"Huh?" Mr. P looked confused.

"Sorry." Zee laughed. "I've got a lot going on, but this helped me figure out a few things."

"Ready to think about music now?"

Zee nodded. "Definitely!"

As soon as the bell rang, Zee hurried to put her guitar away, then raced into the hall. "Chloe!" she called out, trying to catch up with her friends. Jasper and Missy were walking next to Chloe.

Chloe spun around, but when she saw who had called her name, she said, “Oh, I can't really talk. I've got to get to class.”

“I'll walk with you,” Zee said.

“That's . . . not a good idea. You'll be late,” Chloe said.

“But we have the same second-period class,” Zee reminded Chloe. “Come on, let's walk together.” Zee took a deep breath. “I have to tell you and Missy something. I am really, really sorry. That was so stupid of me to criticize your ideas.”

“Really?” Chloe asked.

“Completely,” Zee said. “I mean, there's a reason people love to play those games. I was just feeling guilty for not being there for my mom and you guys, and I took it out on you.” She gestured toward her friends.

“It's OK,” Missy said. “We should have texted you about what we were doing.”

“And I should have said thank you,” Zee told her. “We hardly have any time to get the Baby Blast together! I need as many friends to help me plan it as possible, but you two should be in charge . . . if you want to be.”

Chloe and Missy each gave Zee a hug.

Then Zee turned to Jasper. "And I need to talk to you, too, Jasper."

Jasper's eyes grew wide. "You want me to work on the Baby Blast?"

Zee laughed. "No. My contribution to the science fair project has been a fail so far, but if you forgive me and still want me as a partner, I will do better. I probably won't be able to work on it every single day. But you can count on me to do fifty percent."

"You have a deal!" Jasper said.

"And with Chloe and Missy doing such a fantabsome job on the Baby Blast, I'll definitely have time."

"You can get started today," Jasper said. "Ms. Merriweather said we could work on it in class."

"It's a date!" Zee said. As the words tumbled out of her mouth, her face turned as red as her hair. "I mean . . . you know . . . I'll see you in science."

Then Zee turned on her heel and hurried to her second-period class.

10

Science Friction

Zee stood up from the lunch table and picked up her tray. "I'll see you guys later," she told her friends.

"Where are you going?" Chloe asked. "There are ten more minutes for lunch."

"I know," Zee said, "but I want to get to science a little early, so I can get started on the project." She glanced over at Jasper and thought she saw an *I'm impressed* look on his face.

"Oh, yeah!" Chloe said. "It's such a big project. I want to make a schedule so we can be sure to finish in time."

"How's that going?" Zee asked.

"What?" Chloe asked.

"Having Landon as a partner?" Zee said more quietly

so Landon wouldn't hear.

"Oh, it's fine," Chloe said quickly. "How's your project going, Missy?"

But Zee didn't register Missy's response because she was still focused on Chloe. Zee was certain that she saw a blush in Chloe's cheeks. But she didn't have time to figure out why—she had to get to science.

In the lab, Zee turned on a classroom laptop, then created a Bluetopia doc so that she and Jasper could list ideas then make comments about their pros and cons. They would even be able to edit each other's work right in the document. She was sure that he'd be impressed she had taken the initiative to begin organizing the project.

Before Zee knew it, though, the bell rang and the other students filed in. Conrad and Marcus placed reusable containers filled with lemons, potatoes, nails, and wires on the lab table. Zee knew that they were making batteries from fruits and vegetables. She just didn't realize that anyone had gotten all of their supplies already. Chloe and Landon were laying out a skateboard and helmet, measuring tape, different colors of chalk, and a video camera. Their experiment dealt with the science that makes an ollie, a skateboarding trick, work.

Other partners also had equipment, charts, and books spread out across their tables. Seeing everyone else's progress made Zee worry. They had done so much in just one day! Then Jasper came into the room, with Kathi by his side. Kathi talked quickly as she followed Jasper to his spot at the table next to Zee. "So Ms. Merriweather said we could freeze the balloons in the school's kitchen freezer."

Frozen balloons? Zee thought to herself. *That doesn't sound very scientific.* "What's your project?" Zee asked Kathi.

"Oh, hi, Zee," Kathi said fake-sweetly. "It might be hard for you to understand."

Zee just looked at Kathi, waiting for an answer.

Jasper turned to Zee. "Kathi and Jen are examining how a comet's size affects how quickly it melts," he explained. "Their experiment is really quite brilliant!"

"Do you know what a comet is, Zee?" Kathi asked.

Zee wasn't sure what a comet was *exactly*. But she wasn't going to admit it to Kathi.

Zee looked from Kathi to Jasper, then back to Kathi, when Jasper jumped in to save her. "Of course Zee knows that comets are frozen lumps of gas and rock that orbit the sun," he said.

“Yup,” Zee said quickly.

“Mmmhmm,” Kathi said as she crossed her arms and looked from Jasper to Zee. Zee telepathically thanked Jasper, but she also wondered why she liked that he came to her defense. Was it because she was his partner? His friend? His crush?

“Hey! There’s Jen.” Zee pointed to the door.

Jen struggled to lift two heavy bags.

“So we filled balloons with water, rocks, and sand. Then we froze them,” Kathi went on.

“And Jen is carrying the frozen balloons now?” Zee asked.

“Uh-huh,” Kathi said, nodding.

“Should we help her?” Jasper asked, looking concerned.

Kathi flicked her hand. “Oh, she’s practically at the table. I’ll just wait until she puts all the stuff down there.”

“Well, Jasper and I need to get started on our project, so . . .”

Kathi looked down at Zee. “That’s a good idea. I heard you haven’t really gotten much done yet.” Then, to Zee’s relief, she walked away.

Swiveling around to face Jasper, Zee asked, “Where do we start?”

“Well, I suppose we should start by figuring out the *sort*

of project we should do."

"You mean, like astronomical or physical science?" Zee said, thinking about Chloe and Kathi's projects.

"Precisely," Jasper said.

Then they talked about their ideas. Jasper suggested something with soccer, but Zee didn't think she knew enough about the sport to do that. "Besides, Chloe and Landon are doing something sporty."

Zee suggested fashion, but when Jasper asked her how that could be scientific, her mind went blank.

They went back and forth a few times until Jasper said, "How about music?"

Zee thought about her guitar. "You mean, like how sound is created from vibrations?"

"Or how music affects people's brains."

"Cool beans!" Zee said. "I *love* that idea. Let's do that."

"I suppose we should start by thinking about ideas for specific experiments."

Zee began clicking on the laptop keyboard, pleased that she had already found a website that organized ideas by topic.

Jasper peered over her shoulder. "This is quite comprehensive," he told her. "I'm certain we will find something that suits us."

Trying to hide her smile, Zee began clicking on links and reading the experiment descriptions.

Peeking over the top of the screen, Zee could see Mrs. Sayles, the school secretary, enter the classroom and whisper into Ms. Merriweather's ear. When Mrs. Sayles turned and left, the science teacher looked directly at Zee. "Zee, please gather your things together and go to the main office."

"Won't I come back to class?" Zee asked.

Ms. Merriweather shook her head. "I don't think so."

Zee turned to see practically every student staring at her.

"I'm *so* sorry," Zee mouthed to Jasper as she gathered her belongings. She felt guilty about abandoning him again. But mostly, she was scared. Why did she have to go to the main office?

Everything began to make sense when Zee saw her father waiting in a chair near Mrs. Sayles's desk. He popped up and rushed toward Zee as soon as he saw her. "I had to pull a lot of strings, but I got you an interview with Jamie Sloan. Zee—congrats!"

"Who's Jamie Sloan?" Zee asked, relieved—again—that her father hadn't come to the school because something bad had happened to her mother, or the twins, or her brother.

"Jamie Sloan is one of the best agents in the business,"

Mr. Carmichael explained as he filled in Zee's name and the time on the school's sign-out sheet.

"This is about the TV show?" Zee asked. She couldn't believe that her parents had lectured her about making school a priority—and now her dad was actually making her miss school. "Can't it wait?"

Mr. Carmichael rushed Zee down the hallway toward the exit. "He has to meet with you now. He doesn't have another appointment in his schedule for weeks." He pushed the door open wide. "I promise it won't happen again."

A couple of hours later, Zee's phone vibrated with a text from Chloe:

>Missy and I are going to the mall to shop for the Baby Blast. Wanna come?

Zee texted back:

>Still at the agent's office. I had 2 leave science for nothing!!
>Uh-oh. What happened?
>Hollywood stuff, I guess.

Before hitting "Send," Zee turned to her father and asked, "Since we don't know if Jamie Sloan is ever going to make it back today, can we leave? I want to meet Chloe and Missy at the mall."

"That would be pretty unprofessional."

"I don't think it would be more unprofessional than making people wait *for hours,*" Zee pointed out.

Zee's father gave her a sympathetic look. "I know it's frustrating, but it's all part of becoming a star."

Zee finished her text to Chloe:

>Maybe I can meet you later, after I finally get out of here.

Chloe messaged back:

>I've got soccer and Missy has a violin lesson l8ter. Next time.

Zee peeked out from under her red bangs and saw Dakota Morning walking into the reception area.

Dakota's face lit up in recognition. "Hey! I know you! You're the girl from the elevator the other day."

Ohmygoshohmygoshohmygosh! Zee panicked in her head.

Dakota Morning actually remembered me! "Uh-huh!" was all she could get out.

"I knew I recognized that uniform—and the way you make it look like a fashion statement." She stuck out her hand and said cheerfully, "I'm Dakota Morning. What's your name?"

"Zee. I'm . . . Zee." She didn't know what else to say. Zee had read practically everything that had ever been written about her favorite actress, so she felt like there wasn't anything she could ask Dakota about herself.

Thankfully, Zee's father went in for the assist. "I'm J. P. Carmichael and this is my daughter, Mackenzie Blue."

"Is Mackenzie Blue your real name?" Dakota asked her.

Zee nodded.

"Well, then you were born to be a star." Dakota leaned closer. "For most people, acting is ten percent style and ninety percent faking it. You've got one hundred percent style, and you don't look like a fake to me. You're the real deal."

Zee kept waiting to wake up from this daydream, but this was reality. She was talking to Dakota Morning!

"You may go right in to see Mr. Sloan," Zee heard the receptionist say. But the receptionist wasn't talking to her—she was talking to Dakota.

Zee watched as Dakota Morning walked toward Jamie Sloan's office door. But she didn't mind waiting a little while longer. After all, one of the most famous actresses in the world was actually talking to her—and making her feel like a star. If she was going to have to wait, she might as well work on her new song.

The earth started spinning
When you started grinning.
It all came together
Let's call this forever
For us.

When Zee got home that night, she immediately logged onto Bluetopia to see what she had missed after she'd left early that day. An invitation to a Baby Blast rehearsal at Chloe's house was waiting for her.

Saturday—Baby Blast Rehearsal
Refreshments and fun after practice.

Yes No Maybe

Chloe had actually invited Zee to a Beans rehearsal even though she wouldn't be performing with them at the Baby Blast! Zee clicked on "Yes."

Figuring Chloe was probably home from soccer practice by now, Zee called her to video chat.

"How did you get your parents to agree to let you have a party?' Zee asked.

"Shhhh!" Chloe put her finger up to her mouth. "It's a rehearsal, just like the invitation said."

"But the invitation said there will be refreshments and fun. That sounds like a party, too."

"You know how serious my parents are," Chloe explained. "I finally figured out that they don't care if I have a party—as long as I don't *call* it a party."

"So this way, everyone is happy," Zee translated.

"Besides, we do need to rehearse."

"That was really nice of you to invite me to the . . . rehearsal . . . even though I'm not going to play at the Baby Blast."

"You're still one of The Beans. And my mom and I want to help you and your mom out as much as possible."

"This is going to be so much fun!" Zee squealed at the screen.

"I know, right?" Chloe beamed, then looked away, nervously. "Oh! I've gotta go. Landon is IM'ing me about the science project."

"Is that working out OK?" Zee asked.

"What?"

"Working with Landon?"

"Oh . . . yeah. I mean . . . yeah." Chloe shrugged. "But . . . um . . . I've got to go."

"Talk to ya later!" Zee said, ending the call. Then she looked at the blank computer screen.

Was there something Chloe wasn't telling her?

Yo, Diary.

Something strange is going on with Chloe. I have a funny feeling (funny weird, not funny ha-ha) that she's not telling me something. Kathi's ignoring Landon so she can flirt with Jasper. Marcus and Conrad are always goofing around together and chose each other as science project partners. And now I'm focusing so much of my attention on the TV show. Who's paying attention to Landon? He used to be the most popular boy in seventh grade. Now he seems kind of alone.

Zee ya later!

11
The Big (Screen) Test

Zee sat in front of the TV on Saturday morning and scooped a spoonful of yogurt with fresh strawberries into her mouth. She barely noticed what was happening on the giant screen, though. All she could think about was the fact that today was the first day she didn't have to think about TV—or her TV show, at least. The week had been filled with appointments, and now she wasn't used to having a day to do nothing. But this day was even better than that. This was the day she was going to hang out with The Beans again.

Out of nowhere, Mr. Carmichael appeared in front of the screen.

"What's up?" Zee asked, surprised.

"Guess who is going to be Jamie Sloan's newest client?" Mr. Carmichael asked, grinning.

"Me?" Zee nearly dropped her bowl. "I can't believe it!"

"I can," Zee's father said. "He knows talent when he sees it. That's why he's the best in the business."

"I thought you said he was one of the best," Zee joked.

"Choosing you as a client made him *the best*."

Zee gave her father a hug.

"He'll contact the show's casting director to find out the audition schedule, but he thinks they'll begin soon." Mr. Carmichael headed to the door. "I better call your grandmother . . . and your aunt Lyn . . . and my assistant will want to know . . ." His voice trailed off as he headed down the hall.

As soon as her father was gone, Zee ran to get her diary.

It's me again, Diary.
Chloe's ~~party~~ rehearsal is today, and I don't want to ruin it by making the day all about me. But getting a talent agent is the most amazing thing that has ever happened to me—besides becoming best friends with Ally, Chloe, and Jasper. And becoming part of The Beans. And finding out I'm going to have two more siblings.

You know what I mean.

It just seems as though everything is going right. I don't want that to end. People say, "You can't have it all," but I think you can. I've got the greatest family (even Adam—shhh!), the most amazing band, the best Hollywood agent, and the best friends. Which is why I'm not going to mess things up today by talking about me. Today is about The Beans—and Chloe's party (shhh! again). And I feel like nothing can go wrong.

Zee

Zee arrived at the Lawrence-Johnsons' house early so she could help Chloe set up for The Beans' rehearsal.

Chloe's mother answered the front door. "Oh, hello,

Zee," Mrs. Lawrence-Johnson greeted her. In her simple orange shift dress, she looked as though she was ready for anything from a picnic in the park to a fancy dinner. A strand of glass beads hung around her neck and she wore a matching bracelet. "I wasn't sure you'd make it to the rehearsal. Chloe told me about all of the good things that are happening for you lately. She says you've been very busy."

"Thanks, Mrs. Lawrence-Johnson. I have been busy—but I'm definitely not too busy for my friends."

"Well, Chloe and I are certainly pleased to help out as much as we can with the Baby Blast. Your parents have always been so kind to us."

Zee wondered if it would be OK to tell Mrs. Lawrence-Johnson her good news about getting a talent agent. She wouldn't be taking the attention away from Chloe since no one was there yet. And she was desperate to tell *someone.*

"I just found out—"

"Awesome! You're here." Chloe rushed into the foyer, grabbed Zee's arm, and started to drag her into the kitchen and down the basement steps. "We have so much to do to set up for the *rehearsal.* We need to make sure everyone has enough to eat and drink while they *rehearse.*"

Zee practically stumbled down the stairs behind Chloe, trying to keep up with her friend. "I think it's nice that your parents are letting The Beans rehearse here," she said once they were downstairs.

"Thank you so much for coming early," Chloe said. "You're like the honorary cohost."

"Really?" Zee smiled. "That's so nice."

Maybe it wouldn't hurt to tell Chloe about Jamie Sloan. Technically, the party hasn't really started, Zee thought. "I got some really great n—"

"I can't believe I'm actually going to have a sort-of party," Chloe bubbled. "My parents have never even let me have a sleepover." Then she paused. "I'm sorry, Zee. I'm just so excited. What were you going to say?"

Looking at Chloe's bright face, Zee knew that this rehearsal was as big a deal for her best friend as her news about having a talent agent was to her. Zee didn't want to distract from Chloe's big day.

"It was nothing," Zee said. Then she helped Chloe get the drinks and snacks ready.

Soon the other Beans began to arrive with their instruments. At first, Zee felt like a part of the group—just like old times. She talked and laughed right along with her friends. It was so much fun to be back with the band and to see everyone having a good time. Even Kathi was being completely normal. Zee noticed that Jasper and Landon were hanging out as though they were good friends. They weren't acting competitive at all.

Then Marcus held up a bread stick. "Hey! Who am I?" he shouted. His mouth formed a large O. Then he said, "Uh-oh, I think I broke a string."

"Marcus!" Missy said in an exasperated voice. "It was *serious*!" She started laughing. Everyone else laughed, too, except for Zee.

"What?" Zee looked from one friend to the next, confused. "I don't get it."

"It was something that happened when we were practicing the other day after school," Chloe explained between giggles.

"How about when Jen's mallet went flying up in the air and got stuck on the ceiling tiles?" Conrad said.

"It nearly hit me on the head," Landon said.

Jen rolled her eyes as she laughed. "Oh, it did not."

Zee was beginning to feel left out of the fun. "How did you get it back?" she asked.

"Chloe went to fetch the caretaker," Jasper explained. "He brought a ladder."

"The caretaker?" Zee asked.

The laughter began to die down.

"He means the custodian," Kathi said. She gave Jasper

a playful swat on the arm. "I keep telling you that, Jasper."

Jasper blushed. "I know. I guess I still need a translator."

Zee felt weird that all of the conversation seemed to be about everything she had missed that week. As the party went on, she felt left out of almost every conversation she tried to join.

"Do you think you should start practicing?" Zee said to Chloe a few minutes later. "You know, so your parents don't get suspicious."

"Oh my gosh!" Chloe said. "I almost forgot! Can you help me tell everyone to get their instruments ready?"

Happy to be a part of the rehearsal again, Zee started on one side of the room while Chloe told the people on the other.

Zee's first stop was Kathi and Jen. "Chloe wants to start rehearsing now," Zee told them. "Can you get your instruments out?"

"Thanks, Zee," Kathi said, then gave Zee a pitying look. "I just think it is so nice that even though it's not your band anymore, you are willing to be like a sort of . . . what's the word?"

"Assistant?" Jen chimed in.

"Yes, that's it!" Kathi said enthusiastically.

Zee decided to move on to Jasper, who was at the snack

table, scooping a mound of dip onto a chip.

"I thought I'd find you by the food," Zee teased. When she realized how much she sounded like Kathi, she immediately turned a deep shade of red. *Ohmylanta!* She thought. *Why am I talking to Jasper this way?*

Although Zee hoped Jasper wouldn't pick up on the flirty tone, when his face started turning the same shade of red and he looked at his feet, she knew he had. "Mmmfffwwmmff," he mumbled, his mouth still stuffed with food.

"Chloe says everyone should get instruments out," Zee speed-said, then found Landon alone, gulping down a soda. Chloe reached him at exactly the same time.

"Hey, Landon!" both girls said together.

Chloe giggled nervously. Landon looked from one girl to the other, and Zee looked at Chloe.

"You can tell him." Both girls spoke at the same time again. "You can tell him." Then Chloe let out more nervous laughter.

Landon looked around. "If you want to tell me that we're starting to rehearse, I got it," he said.

"Cool!" Chloe said, hurrying off to join the others.

Zee's eyes followed her best friend suspiciously. *That was interesting.*

The first song that The Beans played was one that Zee

had never even heard before.

"Oooo, baby!" Kathi sang brightly. "When you smile, baby, you make me smile, too." The other band members rocked and played their instruments until the chorus, when they all chimed in for the refrain.

"It's you, baby. It's true, baby. You make the sun shine, baby. You make the flowers grow, baby. You make me know, baby, everything will be all right."

"That was awesome!" Chloe yelled when the song was over.

"You were perfect, Kathi," Missy said, lowering her violin from her chin.

"I think we were all kind of perfect," Conrad said.

Suddenly, everyone turned to Zee. She felt as though a bright spotlight was shining down on her.

"Well, Zee, what did you think?" Kathi asked.

Zee forced a smile across her face. "It's a really fun song," she said. "Did you write it, Kathi?"

Kathi nodded and smiled proudly. "I thought that since you aren't writing any new songs for your mother's shower, I would."

Zee wanted to be polite, but Kathi was actually trying to embarrass her in front of The Beans! She bit her tongue and asked, "So, the 'baby' is an actual baby?"

Kathi rolled her eyes and looked at the other band members. "Obviously."

"It's just kind of obvious to sing about a baby at a baby shower," Zee shot back. Immediately, she regretted it.

Kathi planted her hand on her hip. "What's that supposed to mean?"

"A lot of songwriters work really hard to get simile and metaphor into their songs," Zee explained, trying to backpedal. "It just doesn't seem like . . . that's what you were going for?"

"You don't like our song?" Chloe asked.

"It's not that I don't like it," Zee said. "You guys *sound* fantabsome."

"Then what's your problem?" Kathi said.

Zee looked from one band member to the next. Kathi looked angry, but the others just looked curious—and confused. Even though Zee didn't like the way Kathi insinuated that she had to step in to write songs for Zee's mom's shower, she hadn't meant to offend anyone else.

"It's definitely a really cool song. But I'm not sure it's right for the Baby Blast." Zee spoke slowly so she could choose each word carefully. "You know—it's not supposed to be a typical baby shower."

"I don't think most baby showers have a live band," Jen said.

"With songs written just for the event," Conrad added.

"Maybe you could be a little more appreciative, Zee," Kathi said.

Zee looked at the floor. Why had she let Kathi provoke her? Her friends were doing something *nice* for her.

Kathi's voice pulled Zee out of her thoughts. "I *said*, 'Are you going to get that, Zee?'"

"Huh?" Zee asked.

"Your phone keeps vibrating, Zee," Chloe told her. "We can hear it making noise."

"Oh, yeah." Zee glanced at the iPhone screen. It was a text from her father.

>Urgent: You have an audition in an hour.

Zee typed:

>2day? I thought I would get more coaching before the audition.
>They just want to meet you and a get a sense of what you can do.
>I'm @ Beans rehearsal. It's Saturday!
>Hollywood never sleeps. LOL.

Zee groaned. She had told her parents she didn't really like it when they used "LOL" or "OMG" in their texts. Clearly, her father wasn't getting the message. Zee texted her dad:

>I need 2 change. Can u come get me now and take me home?

As Zee typed her messages, she looked up to see that the band had forgotten about her and was discussing the next song. Everyone was getting along—and going along—with Kathi.

Zee wondered if it would have been better if she hadn't

come to the rehearsal. It seemed as though no one wanted her there. She was relieved when Chloe came over to her.

"Is everything OK?" Chloe asked. "You look upset."

"My dad needs to take me to an audition for the show," Zee explained.

"That's awesome!" Chloe cried.

"I guess," Zee said. "I wish I didn't have to leave."

"But that is so exciting for you—your first *real* audition," Chloe said. "And we're just going to be practicing. Since you're not going to be playing with us . . ."

"Yeah, it's really no prob if you go," said Kathi, who had been listening to their conversation. "We've got everything under control here."

Zee knew Kathi was right. "I'll wait for my dad outside," she said. She got up and left as Kathi counted off for the next song.

When Zee arrived at the audition, she was surprised to see so many other girls around the same age and height as Zee in the lobby. A lot of them even had red hair and freckles.

"I thought they wanted *me* for the part," Zee whispered to her father.

"They're considering a few girls," Mr. Carmichael told her. "Obviously, they like your look. Pretend that they don't

exist and that you're the only one here."

How could Zee pretend they weren't there? The way they were practicing their lines, warming up their voices, and stretching gave Zee the impression they had been to auditions before. Zee tried to do exactly what they were doing, but while they seemed professional and polished, she felt like she was a clown trying out for the circus.

Zee watched as girls left to go into the audition room then came out a few minutes later. Some smiled. A few cried. But Zee wasn't sure if that was all an act, too.

"Just remember that what *isn't* in the script is as important as what *is*," Zee's dad said. "Let's practice your introduction."

"How could I mess *that* up?" Zee asked.

"You'll be nervous," Mr. Carmichael reminded her. "The more you practice, the better."

Zee took a deep breath. "I'm Mackenzie Blue Carmichael."

"And?" her dad prompted her.

"And . . ."

"Thank you for this wonderful opportunity."

"Thank you so much for this wonderful opportunity."

"Nice ad lib!" Mr. Carmichael said, winking.

Zee grinned. "Thanks!"

"I'd give you the part just for that!"

"I wish you were the one making the decision."

"I do, too, but I know they'll see how special you are."

"You may go in, Ms. Carmichael," the receptionist called out.

It took Zee a couple of beats before she realized she was "Ms. Carmichael." No one had ever called her that.

Zee stood up and looked down at her father. "Are you coming with me?" she asked.

Mr. Carmichael shook his head. "I wish I could, but I'll be stuck out here—with my fingers crossed for you."

As Zee walked toward the room where the auditions were being held, the script that she was holding in her right hand shook. She grabbed it with her left hand, too, but then it just made twice as much noise. So she tucked it under her arm and pressed her arm tight against her body.

Zee surveyed the room. There was an older man with a gray-and-black beard, a woman with dark-framed glasses, a man her father's age in a black stocking cap sitting behind a camera, and a guy in the corner eating a sandwich. Besides the cameraman, Zee wasn't sure who anyone was.

At first, no one said anything. Once Zee figured out that they were waiting for her to do something, she smiled and said, "Hi, I'm Mackenzie Blue Carmichael." Then she

handed out copies of her headshot and résumé to everyone in the room, including the man with the sandwich, who pushed the photo out of the way.

"Hi, Mackenzie, I'm Marco Basile, the casting director," the bearded man told Zee. Then he pointed to the woman in the glasses. "This is Lola Monroe, *Rock On*'s director." Zee hoped he would tell her who the man eating the sandwich was, but he didn't.

"*Rock On?*" Zee asked.

"That's the working title for the pilot," Lola Monroe explained.

Duh, Zee told herself, then she remembered what she and her father had rehearsed.

"Thanks so much for this great opportunity," Zee said. *Whew!* She got the entire sentence out without stammering. And so far, she hadn't tripped and fallen down.

"Have you ever acted before?" Marco Basile asked Zee.

"No. Umm . . . I mean, yes . . . but not professionally." *Ohmylanta! Here we go.* Zee wasn't sure how many questions she would be able to make it through.

"How old are you?" the director asked.

Yay—an easy question! "I'm twelve."

"Do you play an instrument?"

"What other experience do you have?"

"What are your goals as a musician?"

The questions came quickly, like fireworks bursting one after another into the sky, but Zee had no problem answering each one.

"Do you need any time to study the sides?" Marco Basile asked.

Was that a trick question? "The sides?" Zee asked.

"The part of the script you'll be reading from," he said.

Zee shook her head. Taking more time to study the script meant more time to get nervous, and Zee didn't want that. "I'm OK. I read through it while I was waiting."

"Great! My assistant, Clark, will be reading with you," Marco said.

The sandwich eater stood up and walked toward Zee. When he was in place, Mr. Basile said, "Go."

Zee started reading from the script. Clark read the

part of Zee's character's best friend, Maddy, delivering his lines as if he were sleepwalking, but Zee got into character completely. When they were finished, she was sure it went really well.

Until the casting director told her to try it again.

"This time, don't get quite so upset when Maddy gives you the news. Remember, she's still your best friend."

Zee started over, keeping his comments in mind as she read. And when he told her to be more forceful at the end of the scene, she read it again. And again, with more anger in the beginning. And then with more forcefulness throughout.

After all of the readings, Zee was surprised to look up and see the smiles on everyone's faces. "Very impressive," Mr. Basile said as Ms. Monroe nodded her approval. "We are looking for a real girl that viewers can relate to," he continued. "You may not have a lot of acting experience, but you have a genuineness about you."

"I do?" Zee asked, surprised that they weren't rushing her out the door.

"And you take direction very well," the casting director added.

Lola Monroe pointed to Zee's clothes. "Which stylist did you use?"

Zee was wearing a skirt she had patched together from pieces of old dresses she had bought at the thrift shop. On top, she wore a loose peach sweater. Zee had hand-sewn tiny sequins across the front of the sweater to create a flower. Her purple Converse high-tops with the shimmering silver laces went nearly up to her knees. "Oh, I picked this out myself. It was kind of last minute, though, because—"

"This is *exactly* what we imagine your character wearing," Mr. Basile said, cutting her off. "Thanks for coming in, Mackenzie. We'll be in touch."

Zee thanked everyone, then hurried out of the room before they could change their minds. *We'll be in touch*, she repeated in her head over and over.

Hi, Diary.

Mom always says life is full of ups and down. I think I got a lifetime's worth in one day.

Hung out with Beans at Chloe's House

Felt like I didn't know what anyone was talking about

Got to hear what the Beans are playing at Baby Blast

Didn't like what I heard

Had an amazing audition

Lots of other girls were auditioning for the same part

I don't know what the rest of the ride looks like, but I hope that there are more highs than lows. (That would be a horrible roller coaster ride, but it would be a great year!) If that's impossible, I guess I won't care . . . as long as the ride is exciting!

Wheee!,

Zee

12

Do-over

Sorry, Diary!

I know it's been a week since I wrote. It's definitely NOT on purpose. It's been CRAZY!

Luckily, no one was mad at me about what I said at the rehearsal at Chloe's house. Except maybe Kathi, but I'm used to that. ☺

I spent almost ALL of this week in acting and singing lessons (when I wasn't in school or doing homework). I've also been working on writing and performing original songs for the next audition, so when I didn't have lessons, I practiced after school with Mr. P. He's had a ton of great suggestions!

I'm exhausted. Still, I appreciate all of the extra help I've been getting, thanks to Dad.

Sleepy Zee

Adam stood over his sister's bed. "Wake up!" he said loudly.

Zee rolled over and opened one eye. Adam was already dressed. "Uh! Don't you know how to knock?"

"Yes, I do. That's what I've been doing for the past five minutes, but since I don't have all day, I decided to try this."

"Why?"

"Dad wants me to drop you off at your voice lesson on my way to meet my AP literature study group."

"What day is it?" Zee asked.

"Saturday."

"Don't I get a day off?" Zee asked, pulling the covers over her head.

"Ask your manager."

"My manager?"

"The one in the kitchen eating breakfast and working on your schedule," Adam said. "Now hurry up. I have to be at the library in thirty minutes."

Pushing the covers down, Zee sat up and sighed. As happy as she had been after her audition, she knew she was up against some really tough competition. She wanted to be ready when she got called back for the next audition.

Zee headed to the kitchen and met her father on the stairs. "There she is!" Mr. Carmichael said, beaming. "America's next musical sensation."

"What do I have besides my voice lesson today?" Zee asked.

Zee's father shrugged. "Nothing—the day is all yours."

"Mine?" Zee asked. "No other lessons?"

"No other lessons. No auditions. No meetings."

"Cool beans!" Zee cried.

She knew *just* what she wanted to do. Juggling all of her school and TV obligations meant that Zee hadn't gotten to see her friends as much as she wanted to. Unless another Hollywood emergency came up, Zee would finally have a chance to hang out with her friends like she used to. She texted Chloe and Missy.

>Can you come for a sleepover tonight?

Within a minute, the responses came back.

>Yes!

>Definitely!

Hiya, Diary.

I am in such a good mood!

I've already been putting a lot of work into being a great actress. Tonight I want to focus on being a great daughter (by FINALLY working on my mother's shower) and a great friend (by hanging with Chloe and Missy).

I can't wait!

Zee

"Let's work on Baby Blast decorations!" Zee suggested as she opened her bedroom door later that evening. "I know my mom would really love it if we made the decorations ourselves."

Three different kinds of paper in a rainbow of colors, a few pairs of scissors, glue sticks, tubes of glitter and sequins, and fabric surrounded the girls.

"Good gosh, Zee," Chloe said. "It looks as though an arts and crafts store exploded in your room."

Missy surveyed the contents of the floor. "Is your mother planning on having any more babies? I think there's enough here for three Baby Blasts."

Zee laughed and picked up a ribbon from one of the piles. "I wanted to give us some options—you know, so that we could all suggest ideas."

zee's room
fluffy stuff

"Well . . . I do have one that I think would be really cool," Chloe said, then looked at Zee. "And different."

"Whatever you think would be good is fine with me," Zee told her. She was going to be super-careful not to be bossy tonight. She was determined to make Chloe and Missy feel like their ideas were important and appreciated.

"How about if we make giant pom-poms out of crepe paper and hang them from the ceiling?" Chloe suggested.

"Cool beans!" Zee said.

Missy grabbed a bunch of fabric. "And we could make fabric tassels out of this material," she added. "Instead of doing everything blue and pink, we could match the pom-poms to the colors in the fabrics."

Zee knew her friends were making an extra effort to come up with ideas that she would like. Luckily, Zee didn't have to fake her enthusiasm since Chloe and Missy really had come up with great ideas.

The three girls began to fold and twist and cut.

"So give us the dirt, Zee," Chloe said. "Is Hollywood as cutthroat and nasty as the magazines say?"

"Actually, everyone I have met has been really nice," Zee answered with a shrug.

"That's so cool," Missy said. "You must be *so* excited all the time."

"It's fun, but I really miss seeing all my friends too," Zee said honestly.

"Can we come to the set of the show?" Chloe asked.

Zee giggled. "I'll make sure my agent puts it in my contract!"

"Will you get to go to the Oscars and the Emmys?" Missy asked.

Chloe held a tube of glue up to her mouth as if it were a microphone. "Excuse me, Ms. Carmichael. Who are you wearing on the red carpet today?"

Zee gave her hair an exaggerated flip. "Well . . . the blouse is Brookdale Thrift Shop. I made the skirt out of a pair of my mother's old blue jeans. And of course, the shoes are by the unmistakable designer Con*versé*." She said the brand name with a heavy French accent.

"Oh la la!" Chloe said in a fake snobby voice as she pretended to look into a camera. "Dakota Morning, eat your heart out!"

Missy laughed. "So many celebrities are so fake. I can't imagine Zee ever becoming like that."

"Ohmylanta!" Zee said. "If I ever do, please tell me."

"Oh, we will," Chloe said, nodding her head.

Zee opened up the sections of the pom-pom she was working on. "This is so much fun. I really miss being with you guys—and The Beans."

"Yeah, it's kind of weird rehearsing without you," Chloe said.

"I'm really sorry about abandoning the band," Zee said. "It must be awful being led by Kathi."

"Kathi's not so bad," Missy said as she evened out the bottom off her fabric tassel with scissors.

"Really?" Zee was shocked.

"Uh-huh," Chloe told Zee.

"Isn't she acting bossy?" Zee asked.

"She's supposed to be. Mr. P put her in charge," Missy pointed out.

"She's actually got really good ideas," Chloe added. "And she's an awesome singer."

"Now that you're busy with the TV show, it's good that there's someone who can take your place," Missy said matter-of-factly.

Zee waited, hoping one of her friends would say something like "Not that anyone could take your place," but neither girl did. The silence was almost as hurtful as Missy's actual words had been. Did she know how much her comment stung?

As she watched Chloe and Missy work on Baby Blast decorations, Zee was certain she was being too sensitive. But there was one more thing that was bothering her.

"Poor Jasper," Zee said, trying to sound casual.

"Why?" Missy asked.

Zee shrugged. "It's just . . . Kathi is always hanging around with him now. Don't you think that's kind of weird since she's always been kind of nasty to him?"

"Maybe Kathi figured out that he's actually really cool and that she should be nicer to him," Chloe said.

Zee focused on the pom-pom in her hands. "It seems like she's flirting with him. Do you think he likes her like that?"

"I doubt it, but it's cool that he's getting more attention," Chloe answered. "And it's awesome that she *clearly* likes him."

What did Chloe mean by stressing *clearly* like that? Was she accusing Zee of sending Jasper confusing messages? It was like she had taken a giant rubber stamp and stamped the word *guilty* across Zee's forehead! Somehow Kathi had managed to spoil her sleepover, and she wasn't even there!

* * *

Zee had a great time with Chloe and Missy—even though Chloe's comment nagged at her until she fell asleep. When they woke up the next morning, the uncomfortable feeling hadn't gone away. After the girls left, Zee knew she needed Ally more than ever. She grabbed her laptop, got comfortable on her bed, and Skyped her BFF. She was relieved when Ally's face appeared on the screen.

"Hey, Zee!" Ally called through the screen.

"Happy Sunday!" Zee called back. "Wait—is it still Sunday in Paris? Wait—are you in Paris right now?" Ally's parents were journalists who traveled a lot, and Ally sometimes traveled with them.

"I am in Paris, and the last time I checked, it was still Sunday." Ally laughed.

"I can hardly keep track anymore," Zee said. "Every day seems crazier than the one before."

"You better get used to it," Ally warned. "That's how it's going to be when you're famous."

"I don't know if I really want to be famous," Zee answered,

throwing her head back on the pillow.

Ally looked hard at Zee through the screen. Zee knew that Ally could tell something wasn't right.

"Why are you upset?" Ally asked.

Zee spilled. "My sleepover with Missy and Chloe wasn't like it used to be. And when I hang out with The Beans, it's not the same."

"But they're *good* changes for the most part, right?"

"Everything is changing so fast. I don't know." Zee paused, then went on. "And I never even get to hang out with Jasper anymore."

"Are you still friends?" Ally asked.

"Of course, we're still friends!"

"Does he know that?"

"We're working on a science pro—" Zee stopped. "Uh-oh."

"What?"

Zee covered her face in her hands, then peeked out at Ally. "I haven't been the best science partner in the world," she confessed.

"How come? Is it just because you've been so busy?"

How did Ally always figure out everything so fast? "It might be because I'm avoiding him. And I can't stand the thought of him having a crush on Kathi," Zee admitted.

"You need to fix it, Zee," Ally advised. "Jasper's one of your best friends. You don't want to mess that up."

"You're right!" Zee said, more determined than ever to make things with Jasper right again. "As soon as we log off, I'm going to make time for us to work on the project together."

"You're welcome!" Ally called.

Zee blew a kiss at the computer screen. "Love ya!"

I've been trying to understand
The way I feel when I hold your hand.
I'm so sure yet I'm so confused.
When you're away I don't know the truth.

13

Mind Over Matter

"I realized that the most successful project will be the one that the judges find accessible and directly useful," Jasper told Zee later that afternoon. She had arranged to meet him at his house, and he was catching her up.

"So I designed an experiment that could be used in virtually any classroom. It tests whether taking exams while listening to classical music can improve students' test scores," Jasper explained.

"Cool beans!" Zee said. "I feel bad that I didn't really help with the idea."

"Actually," Jasper began, "you did."

"Really? How?"

"Remember when we were riding our bikes to school

with Chloe, and you said that everyone likes some kind of music?"

A smile crept across Zee's face as she began to catch on.

"You also mentioned that music affects mood," Jasper continued. "That made me wonder—"

"—if it affects mood enough to make a stressful situation better—like taking a test!"

Jasper pushed his glasses higher on his nose. "Exactly!"

"How do we prove it?" Zee asked.

"Well, since that is just the hypothesis, I am not sure we *will* prove it."

"Got it. So we have to get a bunch of students to take an exam with classical music playing and other students to take it with no classical music playing," Zee said. "How are we going to do that?" Zee wondered aloud.

"We have a test coming up in Mr. Zona's math class. He has several seventh grade math sections, so I have asked him to play music for some of his students and not for other students."

Zee caught on. "So he'll give the tests to some of his students with no music playing and to some of his students with music in the background," she said.

"Precisely!" A huge smile spread across Jasper's face. It had been so long since Zee had seen him smile without looking nervous. She started to get that feeling in her stomach that is sort of a combination of what you feel when you're watching a scary movie or opening up a present. In other words, it was a completely confusing feeling.

Zee snapped back into science mode. Ally was right—Zee did not want to ruin her friendship with Jasper, no matter what happened between the two of them.

"We need to figure out what other factors might affect results," Jasper continued, "so we can exclude any variables."

"Like whether students take the test before or after lunch?" Zee half asked and half suggested.

"Exactly!" Jasper wrote Zee's idea down in his notebook. "Let's come up with some other variables."

Jasper responded enthusiastically to all of Zee's ideas. But the more Jasper told Zee her suggestions were "magnificent," the more Zee wondered if Jasper was saying those things as a science partner or a friend. Zee knew he'd been thinking about this project a lot more than she had.

"We'll need to give Mr. Zona very clear instructions on how to administer the tests to make the process as standard as possible," Jasper said.

Hoping to keep her mind off of her feelings for Jasper and on science, Zee volunteered to work on instructions. "Right!" Zee agreed. "I can write those down for him, so we can just give him a list."

After Zee had written a few lines, Jasper pointed to her notebook. "Didn't you mean to write 'It is necessary' here rather than 'It is *not* necessary'?"

Zee looked at the item where Jasper pointed. *It is not necessary for every student in each group to take the test at the same time.* "Uh, yeah," she said. "I guess that wouldn't work—unless it was Opposite Day." She laughed nervously and crossed out the word *not*.

Jasper tapped his chin with his pencil. "Should the music begin before students come into the classroom or right before they begin the test?"

"Before they come in. That way, Mr. Zona can talk to them about it before the test starts if they have any questions." Zee was pleased that she had a good reason for her choice.

"Brilliant!" Jasper said.

Zee wrote, *Begin to play the music after students enter the classroom.*

"Oh, look," Jasper said, pointing to the word *after*. "I think it's another Opposite Day instruction."

"Sorry," Zee apologized, replacing *after* with *before*. "I guess I need a break from science." It was clear that Zee was not going to do a very good job as long as Jasper was sitting right beside her. She began gathering up her papers and notebooks. "I'll work on this some more at home and put it in a Bluetopia doc for you to check out before we send it to Mr. Zona."

"Are you sure you need to leave straightaway?" Jasper looked as confused as Zee felt.

"Yeah—I'm . . . um . . . not really thinking . . . clearly. I'll work on the list for Mr. Zona and share it with you later today. I promise." Zee headed toward Jasper's front door.

"And I will outline the different ways that the data can be analyzed and presented," he called behind her.

Zee knew Jasper's work would be perfect. She just hoped her contribution would be worthwhile, too.

Oh, Diary.

All this talk about music and science just reminds me about how much I miss The Beans. I mean, I get to see each Bean practically every day. I even see them practicing together a lot.

But I miss playing with them. Even if (when?) I get the lead in the show, will it be as much fun as it is with The Beans?

And what if I don't? Have I messed everything up with everyone who's important to me? I know that they say it's all OK. But I'm just not sure.

Mom

I told her I would plan her Baby Blast and have done practically nothing.

Dad

Have I created a monster?

Chloe

I feel like I don't know how to talk to her anymore.

Missy

She's doing so much for my mom, and I'd like to be better friends with her—but I'm so busy, I don't know if that can really happen.

Landon

Now that I don't have a big crush on him anymore, I worry that he seems kind of lonely. (At least he has Chloe as his science fair partner.)

Jasper

I need to figure this out—fast!

Help!

Zee

14

Science Test

As soon as Zee got back to her house, she spread her books and notes out on the kitchen table, opened up her laptop, and got to work.

Ding dong!

The doorbell rang before Zee even had a chance to write down the first instruction! As she raced to the front door, she saw her mother slowly waddling down the staircase, gripping the banister tightly.

"I'll get it, Mom!" Zee called. She opened the door to see Chloe and Missy standing on the porch.

"Hi!" Zee said, and then stepped to the side so they could come in the house. "Did you forget something from the sleepover?"

Chloe shook her head. "No, we're here to work on the Baby Blast."

By now Mrs. Carmichael had made it down the stairs. "Hi, girls," she greeted Zee's friends.

"Hi, Mrs. Carmichael," Chloe and Missy said together.

"We're going to put the final touches on the menu and decorations today," Mrs. Carmichael explained to Zee. "Do you have time to help us out?"

"You're working on the Baby Blast?" Zee said, surprised and a little upset she hadn't known about their plans. Of course, Zee wanted to help, too. She peered into the kitchen at the work spread out across the table. Could she put off working on the science project for just a couple of hours longer?

About to tell her mother yes, Zee turned back to the group—and looked directly at Chloe. *It's awesome that she clearly likes him.* Chloe's words from the sleepover repeated in Zee's head. Zee had given Jasper a clear message: she was going to make up for all the work she hadn't been doing on their project. She had to prove to him—and herself—that she would stick to it.

"No," Zee told Mrs. Carmichael. "I have a lot of work to do on my science fair project with Jasper." Then she turned to Chloe and Missy. "Thanks for being substitute daughters for my mom."

Missy smiled. "We could never be your substitute!"

"It takes two of us to fill in for you," Chloe joked, throwing her arm over Zee's shoulders.

Mrs. Carmichael and Zee's friends worked in the TV room, and Zee could hear practically everything they were saying as she worked in the kitchen. They laughed as they decided what games to play and picked out baby pictures of Zee and Adam to display at the party.

It was difficult for Zee to concentrate on science when her friends were having so much fun with her mother.

* * *

That evening, Zee typed the last answer to the last question of homework, printed out the assignment, and put everything away in her messenger bag for the morning. Then she flopped down between her parents on the comfy couch in the TV room and closed her eyes.

"Tired?" Mrs. Carmichael asked.

Zee looked at her mother. "I'm way past tired. What's more tired than tired?"

"Exhausted?" Zee's father asked.

"Keep going," Zee said, shutting her eyes again.

"You should probably get to bed, then," Mr. Carmichael suggested. "I arranged for an acting coach to come to the house at seven tomorrow morning to work with you."

"You mean 'tomorrow *night*,'" Zee corrected him sleepily.

"He couldn't come in the evening, and I didn't want it to interfere with school."

What? Zee tried to reason with her father. "But I won't do well if I'm too tired."

"If you fall asleep now, you'll get a full night's sleep."

In a few moments, Zee had gone from tired to awake to worked up. She couldn't believe this! "Don't you think you're going just a little crazy? Right, Mom?"

Mrs. Carmichael put her hands up in the air as if to

surrender. "Remember? I'm letting you and your dad handle this." She patted her belly. "I'm managing a different situation right now. But I will say—" She paused as if she were choosing her words very carefully. "All I want for all of my children is for them to be happy. And your dad wants the same thing. If you don't want to do this anymore, just say the word."

"Your mother is right," Zee's father agreed. "I want whatever you want." He pulled out his iPhone. "I can cancel tomorrow's appointment."

Zee grabbed Mr. Carmichael's arm. "Wait!" she said. Then, more calmly, she asked, "Can't you just postpone it until later this week?"

"This was really his only time this week, Zee." Her father looked at her.

Zee weighed the risk. "So I might not get to work with him before the next audition?"

"Yes, but I'm sure you'll be fine." Zee's father began typing a text.

Zee's mind flashed to all of the girls waiting in the lobby before her audition. Until that point, she had been pretty sure she would be fine, with or without extra coaching. But all of those Zee look-alikes had a lot more acting experience than she did. Zee knew she wanted to do whatever was necessary to get the role. If that meant waking up early for an acting lesson, that's what she would do.

"I better get to bed!" Zee announced, standing up. "I need to get up early!"

Hi, Diary.

Any idea when the glamorous, FUN part of my Hollywood life is going to begin? OK, I know there has been some fun stuff, but so far, no designers have asked me to wear their clothes, no paparazzi have tried to take my photo, and no one has asked me to ride in a limo (which I wouldn't do because limos waste a lot of gas, but still, it would be nice if someone would ask).

I know that's not really how things work and there's really no such thing as "overnight success." I just wish that the show was a sure thing, so I knew I wasn't spending all of this time chasing something that might not even happen. What if all of the hard work doesn't lead to anything . . . at least, not right now?

I'm usually not a competitive person. Does being famous—or at least, getting famous—mean I have to be? I don't want to be, but do I have a choice? Someone has to lose. I just don't want it to be me.

Zee

Little fingers. Little toes.
Fluffs of soft hair. Button nose.
When you sleep and when you wake,
I'll watch over each breath you take.

15

Special Delivery

"What's up, Brookdale?" Ally's face lit up the computer screen.

"Please don't make me smile," Zee said. "It hurts to smile."

"Why?" Ally asked.

"I spent about a hundred hours with a diction coach this week."

"What's a diction coach?"

Zee wished she could remember a time when she didn't know what a diction coach was. "A diction coach is someone who tells you that you talk wrong and makes you repeat things over and over until your mouth hurts."

"You talk wrong?"

Zee shrugged. "It was a shock to me, too."

"Sounds awful. I talk just like you. I must talk wrong, too."

Zee tried to look stern. "Repeat after me: The jolly collie swallowed a lollipop."

"No, *thanks*," Ally said.

Zee laughed out loud. "Oh my gosh, Ally. You always know how to make me feel better."

"That's what I'm here for," Ally told Zee. Then she asked, "Is everything ready for the Baby Blast tomorrow?"

"Yes! And I can't wait! It really is going to be the best baby shower ever."

"Take tons of pictures!"

"I will. Over and out." Zee waved good-bye.

"Over and out." Ally said.

Both girls signed off.

Zee had woken up early on the day of the Baby Blast so she could enter the latest results from Mr. Zona's exams into the Bluetopia docs she shared with Jasper. Both Zee and

Jasper had worked really hard all week. Zee wanted to make sure she got as much as possible done early, since she'd be spending most of the day at the Baby Blast.

Zee got a glass of orange juice from the kitchen, sat down at her desk, turned her laptop on, and began typing. Still not quite awake, she reached for a piece of paper, and before she knew it, her hand hit the glass of orange juice, and the drink spilled all over her desk.

"Ohmylanta!" Grabbing the towel that was lying on the end of her bed, Zee tried to soak up all of the juice. She was happy to see that her laptop was hit with only a small amount. She quickly wiped off the keyboard, hit "Save," and closed her computer.

I'll work on that later—when I'm more awake, Zee told herself.

Later that morning, the doorbell rang practically nonstop. The caterers and servers came early. Then Zee's girl friends arrived to help set up. Even Kathi and Jen helped hang the homemade decorations and organize the materials for the games.

Mrs. Carmichael sat on the couch and watched the activity around her. "I'm sorry I'm not very useful," she apologized. "I suddenly feel so tired today."

Zee and Chloe slid an ottoman under Mrs. Carmichael's feet. "Don't worry about it, Mom," Zee said. "We're good."

"Besides, you aren't supposed to be helping out, Mrs. Carmichael," Chloe added. "This is your day."

Mr. Carmichael leaned down and kissed his wife good-bye. He and Adam were off to play tennis during the party.

"Have fun, girls!" Zee's dad called. Adam grabbed a piece of shrimp off the table as he followed his father out the door.

As soon as the door shut behind Zee's father and brother, the guests began to arrive. Chloe's and Missy's mothers arrived first, followed by Mrs. Chapman, then a few of Mrs. Carmichael's friends who lived on the block.

The next pair of women was unfamiliar to Zee, although they recognized her immediately.

"I'd know those freckles and red hair anywhere!" one woman announced. "You've had those since the day you were born."

Although Zee liked to stand out in a crowd, she liked it to be because of her musical talent or her fashion sense. *You forgot to mention my flat chest,* Zee wanted to say. *I've had that since the day I was born, too.*

"I'm Joanne O'Neill and this is Monica Flores," the first

woman through the door said.

"From New York City!" Zee cried, realizing who these guests were.

"We've known your mother since we were your age," Ms. Flores put in.

Zee looked across the room at Chloe and Missy and smiled, certain that they would be at Zee's baby shower one day, too.

After all of the guests arrived, Zee joined the other girls in serving refreshments. Kathi and Jen wove through the groups with fruity drinks. Worried she would end up tripping and spilling the glasses all over the guests, Zee volunteered to carry the trays of finger sandwiches.

"Are you having fun, Mom?" Zee asked as she offered Mrs. Carmichael a sandwich.

"I'm having a wonderful time. This is the *perfect* shower!"

Zee smiled. Even though she hadn't planned as much of the Baby Blast as she'd wanted, it had been her idea to have it in the first place. But she was mostly happy that she had such amazing friends who wanted to help and to be a part of her family.

The doorbell started ringing again. When Zee opened the door, she found Landon, Conrad, and Marcus waiting.

"Mmmm," Marcus said, reaching for a finger sandwich.

"I'm starving!"

"Me too!" Conrad said. "Got any peanut butter and jelly?"

Without answering, Zee absentmindedly held out the tray for the boys to take what they wanted. "Where's Jasper?"

Landon shrugged. "He called us at the last minute and said to go without him."

Conrad gulped down his tiny sandwich. "I believe his exact words were 'a crisis of phenomenal proportions.'" He parroted Jasper's British accent.

Zee's eyes grew wide. "Is he OK?"

"He looks all right to me," Marcus said, pointing.

Jasper climbed out of his father's car and hurried up the steps to the Carmichaels' house with a frazzled expression on his face. Although he was perfectly dressed in his usual weekend clothes—crisp khaki pants and a short-sleeve collared shirt—Zee could tell that Jasper was *not* all right.

"What's wrong?" Zee asked him, worried.

"I think you may have erased all of our work on the science fair project," Jasper said.

Zee could tell he was trying to appear calm. What could have happened?

"Well, I'm out of here," Conrad said, heading toward the living room.

"Me too," Marcus said, following him.

Landon looked as though he wanted to stay to hear what was about to happen, but Marcus circled back and pushed him into the living room. "I think I smell shrimp in here, buddy," Marcus told him.

"How could I have erased everything?" Zee asked helplessly. "It was all in our shared documents."

"The documents are all there," Jasper explained. "But they're all blank, and the history says that you were the last person to edit them."

Nothing was making sense. Zee thought back and pictured herself typing on her laptop, entering information into the computer. Then she watched herself knock over the glass of orange juice, frantically wipe the keyboard, and . . . hit "Save" without checking to make sure all of the documents' contents were still there!

"I must have wiped away the information when I wiped up the orange juice I spilled," Zee said out loud—and then

immediately wished she hadn't.

"You hit 'Save' without checking to see what you were saving?" Jasper sounded really angry, even though he still looked calm.

"I have all of the information somewhere," Zee explained. "I can re-create all of the documents."

"I guess that's what you will have to do," Jasper said. "Can you put it back together before the end of the weekend?"

Zee took her right hand away from the tray of sandwiches and held two fingers up in the air. "I promise."

At that moment, Zee's phone rang. As she reached into her pocket to get it, the tray of sandwiches crashed to the floor, ringing out like a gong.

"Dad?" Zee answered the phone as Jasper began picking up the food from the floor.

The rest of The Beans and Mrs. Carmichael hurried over to see what the commotion was about.

"Are you two OK?" Mrs. Carmichael asked.

Zee nodded, then said into the phone, "Today?"

"What is it, Zee?" her mother asked.

"Yeah, what's up?" Chloe said.

The crowd grew curious about Zee's mysterious phone call now that they knew Zee was okay.

Zee pulled the phone away from her face. "They want me to come back for another audition," she said, only half as excited as she should have been. "Right now."

Chloe took a step closer. "What are you going to do?" she asked.

"Should I leave the shower now?" Zee asked her father at the other end of the line.

"It's up to you," Mr. Carmichael told her.

Zee knew he had meant it when he had told her she should continue with the TV pilot only if she wanted to. But if she didn't go to the audition, would she be letting him down after all of his hard work?

Mrs. Carmichael placed her hand gently on Zee's shoulder. "Don't worry about the shower. You'll have a lot of years to celebrate the twins and help me out with the babies."

Zee could feel the weight of her mother's whole body press against her shoulder, as if she needed Zee to hold her up. Zee looked at her mother's tired face.

"What if I don't go?" Zee asked her father.

"I'm not sure," he said. "This may be your only chance to audition again."

Zee looked at her mother, torn. "Are you sure you don't mind?"

Mrs. Carmichael forced a smile. "I'm surrounded by my favorite people in the world." She placed her hand on her heart. "And since I always have you in here, you'll be with us, too."

"I'll be ready when you get here," Zee told her father. Then she hung up the phone and raced to the TV room to find her guitar.

Chloe and Missy followed her. "How can you leave your own mother's baby shower?" Chloe asked Zee.

"My mom said she's fine with it," Zee told her. "I probably won't get another chance to audition."

"And your mother probably won't have another Baby Blast."

Suddenly, the last thing Zee needed was someone else accusing her of not doing her part. "It's really nice that you helped my mom with the Baby Blast, but I need your support, too."

"Missy and I supported you by putting this party together with your mother when *you* didn't have the time to do it!"

Missy stepped forward. "Chloe really was trying to help

out, Zee," she said in her quiet voice. "She did it because you're her best friend."

"Then she should know that the audition is a really big deal for me!" Zee said.

"When have I acted like it wasn't?" Chloe asked defensively.

"Right now!" Zee snapped.

Kathi and Jen stepped into the room, followed by the rest of The Beans. "Just let her leave, Chloe," Kathi said.

"She wasn't planning on playing with the band today, anyway," Jen added.

Zee looked at her fellow band members, then her eyes rested on Chloe and Jasper.

No one said anything. No one came to her defense.

Suddenly, Mrs. Carmichael's voice broke the silence. "Zee, there's something I think you should know," she said. "I've gone into labor."

16

Little Things

As she watched Mrs. Chapman guide Zee's mother to her minivan, Zee called her father.

"What's going on?" Mr. Carmichael answered. "Is everything all right?"

"How did you know something was up?" Zee asked, momentarily distracted from her mom going into labor.

"You never call—just text," he said.

"Well, you're right," Zee told him. "You're going to be a father! I mean . . . you're going to be a father, again! Mrs. Chapman is taking Mom to the hospital right now."

After making sure everyone was all right, Mr. Carmichael said, "Adam and I will meet you there."

The Beans and the rest of the Baby Blast guests climbed

into the other cars and drove toward the hospital. Zee climbed into the minivan with Mrs. Chapman, her mom, Jasper, Marcus, Conrad, and Landon.

Zee was sitting right next to Jasper, who kept typing on his iPad, scratching his head, and muttering to himself. She knew he was worried about the science fair, but at that moment, Zee had too many other things on her mind to try to convince Jasper that she would save the project. The twins were just more important.

The boys may have thought Zee had let The Beans down just as much as the girls did, but they didn't seem to be thinking about Zee now. Even Conrad and Marcus weren't cracking their regular jokes. Zee felt sorry for Landon, who looked terrified—probably convinced Mrs. Carmichael was going to give birth in the minivan before they got to the hospital.

Luckily, that didn't happen. But as soon as they pulled up to the hospital's main entrance, the nurses hurried Mrs. Carmichael to a desk in the maternity ward to check her in. Mrs. Chapman sat with her and helped answer questions.

Zee and the boys went to the nearby waiting room, where some of the other shower guests and The Beans had gathered. Zee looked over at Chloe, who was sitting next to Missy. Neither girl looked up.

Zee was relieved when her dad and Adam arrived. Mr. Carmichael immediately rushed to his wife's side, and Mrs. Chapman and Adam came into the waiting room.

"Zee and Adam, why don't you go see your mother and father?" Mrs. Chapman suggested.

"Are you sure it's OK?" Zee asked, not certain where she was allowed to go in the maternity ward.

Mrs. Chapman nodded.

"Well, your mother gave us a surprise," Mr. Carmichael said to Zee as she and Adam walked toward her parents.

"It's not a total surprise," Zee said, looking sideways at her mother's large belly.

Mr. and Mrs. Carmichael laughed.

"Listen, Zee," her father said seriously. "I'm not going to be able to take you to the audition, but Mrs. Chapman says she is more than happy to."

"Dad, I'm not going," Zee said. Zee had wanted the part on the TV show, but her family was more important.

"I really think you should go with Mrs. Chapman," Mrs. Carmichael said. "You'll probably be able to perform an entire play—with intermission—before these babies are born."

Zee looked from her mother to her father, who was gazing down at her mother. She knew he loved his role as stage dad, but he loved his roles as just plain dad and husband even more. Anyone in the hospital could see that.

When Zee had just left her friends in the waiting room, the tension of the last half hour had been melting away. Conrad and Marcus were high-fiving Landon. Jasper was showing Kathi and Jen something on his iPad. And Chloe was bouncing up and down, excitedly telling Missy something. They all could have gone home, but instead they had come to the hospital to be with Zee's mother.

"I want to stay," Zee said.

"You don't need to do that," Mrs. Carmichael said.

"I know you're not asking me to choose," Zee explained. "But I've learned a lot over these past few weeks."

"You don't want to waste all of what you learned about acting by hanging around and just waiting, do you?" Zee's mother looked concerned.

Zee took a deep breath. "It won't be a waste at all—since the most important thing I've learned is that I don't want to be an actress."

"But, Zee, it was always your dream to be a star!" Mrs. Carmichael said, looking up at her daughter.

"It still is. But if I get the part, it won't be a dream anymore. And now I know that I really want to be a musician, not a TV actress." Zee looked at her father. "I'm sorry. I know you worked really hard for me. But I'm not sure I'm cut out to be on a TV show. I just want to write songs and play in a band with my friends. At least for now."

Mr. Carmichael put his arms around his daughter and pulled her close to him. "The truth is, I don't think I'm ready to be a real stage dad. I just liked acting like one."

Zee looked at her mother, and they shared a secret grin. "You sure are a good actor! You nailed the part, Dad."

* * *

Zee's heart pounded as she walked across the waiting room toward her best friend.

"Hey!" Chloe said brightly.

"Hi," Zee said, then stopped. She was afraid to say anything else just yet.

Then Chloe asked, "Could you play us one of the songs you've been working on for the audition?"

"Really?"

"Sure. You brought your guitar." Chloe pointed to the spot where Zee had put it down across the room.

"Ohmylanta! I guess I was holding it when we rushed to the hospital."

The other Beans gathered around Zee and Chloe. "It looks like we're going to be here awhile," Landon said. "I think we need some entertainment."

"There's a courtyard in the middle of the hospital," Missy's mother said. This was the hospital where she performed surgery. "You can go out there and you won't bother anybody."

"Let's go!" Chloe said, and The Beans followed Missy to the outdoor courtyard.

Zee lifted her guitar out of its case and took a breath.

At first, she sang quietly.

"How can it be? Can it be true? Here I am looking at you."

She had never performed like this in front of The Beans before, and it felt strange to be singing songs she had written to perform by herself. But as they smiled and applauded, Zee grew louder and bolder.

"When you came I couldn't believe that
I'd fall in love. I'm head over heels!"

Continuing to play, Zee watched a few people walk out into the courtyard to hear the music.

"But now that you're here, whatever was true is now
just a lie. I was waiting for you."

By the time she got to the chorus, the crowd had grown larger.

"The earth started spinning when you started grinning.
It all came together. Let's call this forever—for us."

When Zee finished her song, the audience applauded loudly. But she hardly noticed because something else got her attention. Adam and the parents of The Beans were carrying out the band's instruments.

"They were in the cars, so we decided we shouldn't let all of that Baby Blast practicing go to waste," Mrs. Lawrence-Johnson explained.

Chloe wrapped her mother in a hug.

"Yay!" Kathi cheered, rushing to get her violin from Mrs. Barney. "This is going to be The Beans' best performance yet, because I'm singing lead!"

Chloe looked at Zee from behind her cello and rolled her eyes.

"One two three four," Kathi shouted, and The Beans started to play.

Zee stepped aside and watched The Beans perform, just like any other fan. She had to admit that Kathi's voice soared, and the songs she had written with The Beans for the Baby Blast really highlighted it. All of the band's instruments and voices came together—they were fantastic.

More and more people came to the courtyard to watch The Beans. Nurses and other staff members started to bring out patients to hear them. The ones in wheelchairs tapped their hands and feet. The people standing swayed and danced to the music. Some clapped to the beat. It made Zee happy to see that so many other people were enjoying the music.

After The Beans finished their third song, the boys started whispering, then chanting, "Zee! Zee! Zee! Zee!" Soon the girls joined in. Even Kathi was chanting Zee's name! Adam and The Beans' parents added their voices.

Zee grabbed her guitar and rejoined The Beans in the center of the courtyard. "Let's sing something everyone knows." She looked out at their audience. "How about 'Little Things' by One Direction?"

Everyone agreed. Then Kathi stepped backward to make room for Zee—and only pouted a little.

"Are you going to start us off?" Zee asked.

Kathi looked around as if she thought she was the victim of an April Fools' prank. Finally, she asked, "You want me to be the lead singer?"

"You've earned it," Zee said, meaning it.

Kathi placed her violin on her shoulder and pulled her bow across the strings to play the song's introduction. Zee did have to admit that it was kind of nice not having so much responsibility for how the band sounded for once. She could just relax and enjoy being part of the group.

After the band had played the last note and the audience applauded, one set of clapping hands stood out from the rest.

"Dad!" Zee exclaimed, racing over to her father. "How's Mom?"

The rest of the band was right behind her.

"Has Mrs. Carmichael had the babies yet?" Chloe asked.

Mr. Carmichael beamed. "She's had the babies, and everyone is doing great!"

"Are they boys?" Zee asked.

Mr. Carmichael shook his head.

"Girls?" Zee said excitedly, but her dad shook his head again.

"Monkeys?" Conrad guessed from behind Zee, and everyone laughed.

"One boy and one girl," Mr. Carmichael announced proudly.

"What are their names?" Missy asked.

"Phoebe Grace and Connor O'Neal," Mr. Carmichael told them.

"Can we meet them?" Kathi asked.

"Only Zee and Adam will be able to see them today," Mr. Carmichael said. "But from what I hear, The Beans made this the most memorable birth Brookdale Hospital has ever seen."

"You guys definitely made it special for me," Zee told her friends, turning around to face everyone.

"Group hug!" Marcus shouted, and everyone reached their arms out.

After a few moments, Mr. Carmichael asked, "If Zee is somewhere in the middle, could you all let her out? I'd like her to meet her brother and sister before their first birthday."

When Zee finally reached her mother's hospital room, Mrs. Carmichael was holding the twins in her arms and looking down at them.

First Zee hugged her mother, and then she gave each baby a kiss on the forehead. "Hello, Phoebe," she said to the tiny baby in a little pink hat. "Hello, Connor," she said to the tiny baby in a little blue hat.

"How does it feel to be a big sister, Zee?" Mr. Carmichael asked.

Before Zee could answer, Mrs. Carmichael said, "I'm sorry you missed your big chance today, Zee."

But when Zee looked down at her siblings' rosy faces, she knew she would always be a star in their eyes. "If I had gone to the audition, I would have missed this."

Then Zee began singing the song she had been working on the hardest over the past few weeks—a song that had nothing to do with the TV pilot.

It was a lullaby for her brand-new brother and sister.

She whispered sweetly to them:

"Little fingers. Little toes.
Fluffs of soft hair. Button nose.
When you sleep and when you wake,
I'll watch over each breath you take."

Hi, Diary.

You know what's better than having millions of adoring fans? Having two adorable siblings. And lots of amazing friends. And really cool parents. And the best life a girl could possibly ask for!

Zee

Zee closed her diary. The twins and her mother would be at the hospital for a few days, the Baby Blast was over, and she didn't have to prepare for her auditions anymore. Zee logged on to Bluetopia, pulled out her science binder, and got to work retyping all of the information that had disappeared that morning.

17

Chloe's Surprise

Two weeks later, Zee and Chloe chatted online, just like they had every day since the babies were born.

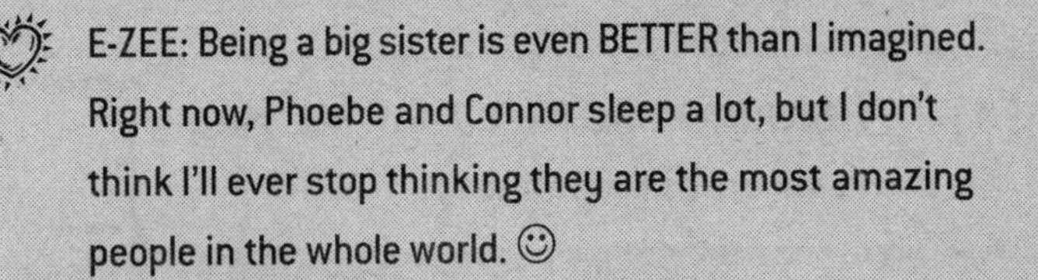

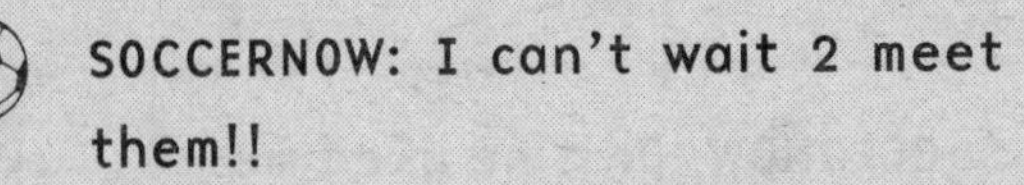

E-ZEE: U R coming over w/The Beans later, right?

SOCCERNOW: R u kidding? But there is something I wanted to tell U first . . .

E-ZEE: ???

SOCCERNOW: I kinda like Landon now.

E-ZEE: No way.

SOCCERNOW: R U mad?

E-ZEE: I think it's awesome!!! Why didn't u tell me b4?

SOCCERNOW: At first I wasn't sure if I liked him that way.

E-ZEE: Sounds familiar. LOL.

SOCCERNOW: Or if he liked me.

E-ZEE: Does he?

SOCCERNOW: Yes! The science project made us see how much we have in common. Plus, he is so cute. What's up with u & Jasper?

E-ZEE: Jasper is one of the best friends anyone could ask 4. & . . . I think it should stay that way. I'm going to tell him later today.

SOCCERNOW: Fingers xed 4 u!

E-ZEE: Thx!!

SOCCERNOW: GTG, but I will C U soon. Can't wait to meet Connor and Phoebe.

"Ta-da!" Zee cried as she pushed open the door to her new bedroom, her girlfriends standing behind her.

"Awesome!" Chloe said.

Zee's new room didn't look anything like her old one. One wall was orange and the other three were a calm pale green. Zee's queen-size bed sat on a simple platform, and small circular orange rugs dotted the floor.

"Look at the windows!" Missy said. "You used the fabric tassels from the shower!"

"And you hung the pom-poms from the ceiling!" Chloe pointed out.

"Pretty cool, huh?" Zee said. "I *never* would have thought of that without you guys."

"It's perfect for you, Zee," Kathi said. Zee knew that coming from Kathi, that was a big compliment.

"What's that?" Jen asked, pointing to the top of the dresser.

"Mr. Sock Puppet!" Chloe exclaimed, laughing. "I can't believe you really gave him a place of honor, Zee."

"What did you think I would do?" Zee asked. "Throw him out?"

"Yup!" Chloe laughed. "That's what *I* would have done."

The doorbell interrupted them.

"The boys are here!" Zee cried, leading everyone back downstairs. When she opened the door, Jasper, Conrad, Marcus, and Landon walked inside.

Landon immediately walked right up to Chloe and started to talk to her. Zee couldn't believe how cute they looked together.

Zee led everyone into the dining room, where snacks had been set out on the table.

"I can't believe your mother did all this with two new babies!" Missy said.

"She didn't do it. I did," Zee said proudly. "I hope you like everything."

"I volunteer to sample everything and let you know," Marcus said.

Everyone started to pile food onto their plates and spread out across the room, eating and laughing. Zee sat next to Jasper, who set down his plate. "There's something in the TV room I want to show you." She gestured for him to follow her to the next room.

"Brilliant!" Jasper exclaimed, right behind her.

When Jasper saw the big poster she had put together for the science fair, he cried, "I *cahn't* believe how *fantastic* it looks!"

"I just printed everything out and pasted it on here,"

Zee said. "You're the one who figured out how to make all of the numbers make sense."

"I think we make a great team," Jasper said.

"I do too. Thanks for putting up with all of my craziness the past few weeks."

"I'm glad I did. I think we really have a shot at going to regionals."

"Yup." Zee paused for a moment. "I'm also sorry for how confusing everything was after Brookdale Day. You are an awesome friend. That's why I'd like to make sure we *stay* friends . . . just friends."

Zee managed to look at Jasper, but before he could respond, Kathi burst into the room. "Are you kidding me?" she cried. "I wasted all that time pretending I liked Jasper, and you didn't even like him that way." She stomped back out again.

"I'm sorry about Kathi, too," Zee said.

"Oh, I do *not* care about Kathi," Jasper said. "I had a

suspicion that's what she was doing the whole time. Still, I was secretly hoping you might get jealous. I guess that was pretty stupid."

"Now we're even," Zee said, smiling.

Then *ooohs* and *aahs* floated in from the next room.

"They are so *adorable*!" Zoe heard Chloe squeal.

"Are you crying, Conrad?" Zoe heard Marcus ask.

"No," Conrad said, sniffling.

Zoe and Jasper burst into laughter. "Come on," Zee said, grabbing Jasper's arm and guiding him back into to the dining room. "I'll introduce you to Phoebe and Connor."

"Well, thanks for letting us know, Jamie," Zee overheard her father say into his phone after all her friends had left.

"Was that Jamie Sloan?" Zee asked when he hung up.

Mr. Carmichael nodded. "He wanted to let us know that they cast the starring role for *Rock On*."

"Who is it?" Zee asked. She couldn't help but be curious.

"Dakota Morning."

"Dakota Morning?" Mrs. Carmichael sounded confused. "I thought they wanted an actor no one had heard of yet."

"Looks like they changed their mind and decided they wanted a super-celebrity," Mr. Carmichael said, shrugging.

* * *

Later on, she Skyped Ally to catch her up on all of the news.

"It's a good thing you didn't leave the Baby Blast to go to that audition," Ally told Zee.

"I almost did!" Zee said. "I guess I got really caught up in the idea of being a star."

"You've always wanted to be a rock star, Zee. And I would have gotten caught up in all of it, too. It seems like such an exciting life."

"It kinda was," Zee told her BFF. "And it kinda wasn't. I'm glad it happened, but for now I'm happy just being a friend and a sister."

18

And the Winner Is...

Hi, Diary.

Ms. Merriweather announced the winner of the Brookdale Academy seventh grade science fair today. That's right! I said "winner," because only one person is going to regionals—Missy. Her presentation was amazing!! I don't think anyone knew how amazingly smart she was until today.

Even though Jasper and I didn't win, I learned a lot from the project. (I think I might have learned more about my friends than I learned about science.)

Anyway, I'm really happy for Missy. I bet she'll win regionals and go on to state. I hope so, because after all she did for me and my mom, I now I consider her one of my very best friends! (What?! You can never have too many best friends!)

Zee

Online Glossary

&	and
@	at
<3 (sideways heart)	= love (<33 = extra love)
=	equal
1	one
1st	first
2	to; two; too
2day	today
2-faced	two-faced
2gether	together
2morrow	tomorrow
2nite	tonight
4	for
411	information
4get	forget
4give	forgive
4gotten	forgotten
ASAP	as soon as possible

b	be
b/c	because
b/f	boyfriend
b4	before
BB4N	bye-bye for now
BFF	best friends forever
bz	busy
c	see
CA	California
cld	could
every1	everyone
g/f	girlfriend
gr8	great
GTG	got to go
GTR	got to run
H&K	hugs and kisses
K	okay
LOL	laughing out loud
LYLAS	love you like a sister
M	am
mayb	maybe
mins	minutes
MUSM	miss you so much
NK	no kidding

no1	no one
NP	no problem
nt	not
OMG	oh, my God
OMGYG2BK	oh, my God, you've got to be kidding
OTOH	on the other hand
pic	picture
pls	please
r	are
rm	room
thm	them
thx	thanks
TTFN	ta-ta for now
u	you
u'll	you'll
ur	your; you're
urs	yours
w	with
w/o	without
WB	write back
WFM	works for me
ws	was
y	why

Curious to know how Zee's story began?
Read on for a sneak peek at her first book,

Hi, Diary,

Today I'm kind of blue. Not blue as in Mackenzie Blue, which I always am. (Ugh! I can't believe I just made that joke.) This kind of blue is so not even funny. Not even a little.

First, my BFF Ally moves ALL THE WAY to PARIS, which is incredibly great for her. Who wouldn't want to live in France? The French have the most fabulous food, très chic fashion, and THE CUTEST guys. (Oooo la la!) Mom says Ally's move could be good for me, too. I'm not sure.

A *ding!* from Mackenzie Blue Carmichael's computer interrupted her. She slipped her diary and pen off her lap and rushed over to her desk. Awesome! An IM from Ally!

SPARKLEGRRL: R u there?

Zee typed quickly.

E-ZEE: Yes. I was just thinking of u!

SPARKLEGRRL: Help! I h8 school! ☹

E-ZEE: What's wrong??!

SPARKLEGRRL: Everything. I can't sleep. No 1 here wants 2 talk 2 me. Maybe it's because I have NO idea how 2 dress like a French person. Did u know they have a thing against sneakers here?

E-ZEE: Making friends isn't easy, especially in a new country!

So true. Zee became great friends with Jasper Chapman after he moved to Brookdale from London, England, over the summer. Jasper told Zee he had been lonely before he met her at the pool. Even with Jasper, Zee still missed Ally. They had been best friends and had gone to Brookdale Academy's lower school since preschool. And Zee needed Ally more than ever now that she was a seventh grader in Brookdale Academy's upper school—in a different building with different teachers.

E-ZEE: I m nervous about my 1st day of school 2.

SPARKLEGRRL: Y?

E-ZEE: What if I can't find my way around? What if I 4get my locker combo? What if my life ends bc all I have time 4 is homework?

SPARKLEGRRL: I know how u feel. I got lost AND 4got my combo. No hw yet tho.

E-ZEE: Ugh! Being a 7th grader in Upper is like being a kindergartner

in Lower. U r 1 of the little kids—
except no 1 thinks u r cute.

SPARKLEGRRL: At least you are not alone. Like me.

E-ZEE: No, u r not. U have me. BFF!!!!

Zee looked at the clock on her computer.

E-ZEE: OMG! G2G! Time for school!

SPARKLEGRRL: OK. LYLAS.

Zee grabbed her diary and dropped it in the black book bag that she'd decorated with pink and yellow felt flower cutouts. *I'll finish writing in my diary on my way to school,* she decided. As she walked downstairs, she texted Jasper on her Sidekick, which she'd covered with a bright blue skin that had a big pink Z in the middle.

>Want 2 meet up outside b4 school?

she typed on the keypad. Zee was new to the upper school, but Jasper was new to Brookdale Academy. He didn't know his way around at all.

His response came back right away.

>Sure.
I'm leaving now.
C u soon.

As Zee's dad drove her to school, Zee began a list of what was good and bad about Ally's living in France.

Good

1. I get to visit my BFF in France! (My parents already promised!)

2. I'll get a sneak peek at the newest French fashions before they come to LA!!

3. She can teach me French, and we can talk "in code" when I don't want my parents to know what I'm saying.

Bad

1. I'm miserable without my BFF here.

2. Ally's in a completely different time zone. What if I need her when she's sleeping—or she needs me when I'm at school?

3. What if Ally finds a new best friend in France?

Unfortunately, thanks to that last "bad," I think Mom might be wrong. Ally's move is still AWFUL!! ☹

And then there's my other big problem. But in this case, not so big. That's what makes it a problem. You know how most girls my age start getting boobs? Well, my body has decided to put all its energy into adding freckles to my face instead.

I probably just got three more freckles while I was writing that.

Zee

Zee closed her diary, slid the clasp into the latch, and put it back in her book bag. Then she looked out the SUV window.

"Dad, you can just stop the car now!" she said a little louder and more panicked than she'd meant to.

"But we're still a block from school, Zee," her father said. "I can't just leave you here on your first day."

"But I *want* you to."

J.P. Carmichael's right eyebrow rose up on his forehead, the way it always did when he was suspicious. "Why?" he asked.

"I don't want you to go out of your way."

"It's no problem," Zee's father said. "In fact, it's easier for me to just turn around in the school's drop-off circle."

Zee let out a deep sigh. "Dad, *please* stop the car."

Mr. Carmichael slowed down and steered to the curb. "Come on, Zee. What's going on?" he asked.

"It's your car, Dad," Zee explained. "It's kind of embarrassing." Zee had hoped to get a ride in her older brother's sporty red subcompact, but as usual Adam had overslept and was still shoveling corn flakes into his mouth when she was ready to go.

"You're embarrassed to be seen in a brand-new SUV?" he asked. "Would you prefer an ancient clunker with duct tape holding on the bumper?"

"What kind of gas mileage does the clunker get?" Zee asked.

Mr. Carmichael put his hand on his daughter's arm. "This isn't about the car, sweetie. You're just nervous about school. Don't worry—it will practically be the same as last year."

"Well, last year it was still a green school. You know, save the planet and end global warming so that your children will actually be able to breathe without a gas mask when they get older?" She opened the door, slid out of her seat, and planted her orange Converse high-tops on the sidewalk.

Mr. Carmichael sighed and ran his hand over the passenger seat. "But it's soooo comfortable."

"Sorry, Dad. I have to protect the family's reputation," Zee told him.

"But I am family."

"Yeah. And you're *kind of* making the rest of us look bad." She shut the door and gave her father a smile.

Mr. Carmichael hit the button to lower the automatic window. "Have a great first day, honey," he said.

"Thanks, Dad," Zee said, turning toward the school.

She had taken only a couple of steps when she heard her father shout. "Hey, Mackenzie!" Zee's dad called her by her full name only when he was working hard to stay calm.

"Yes, Dad?" Zee said super-sweetly, spinning around and preparing for whatever was coming. Her father's eyebrow was up again.

"I think maybe the school gave you the wrong size uniform," he said. "Your skirt seems a little short."

Zee didn't bother to look down. She knew the exact length of her skirt. In the lower school, they had worn white blouses under blue plaid jumpers that hung nearly to their knees, but now that Zee was in seventh grade, she got to mix and match school-issued skirts, shirts, and sweaters. Although the pieces would never be trendy, they were way better than what she had had to wear to school before. And Zee planned to make the uniform—and herself—stand out. That meant wearing her sneakers, cool patterned socks, colorful beaded necklaces, bracelets, and earrings that she'd made herself—and shortening her hem.

"My skirt's fine," Zee said. "It just can't be any higher than my fingertips." She held her arms by her sides to demonstrate.

Mr. Carmichael squinted. "I think you might be bending your elbows a little," he said doubtfully.

Sighing, Zee stood at attention and stretched her arms down as far as they would reach. "See, Dad? Nothing to worry about. Totally regulation length. Mom hemmed it herself."

"At ease, soldier." Zee's father blew her a kiss. "Company dismissed."

"See ya!" Zee shouted with a big wave. She stuck her earbuds in, turned up her iPod, and made her getaway down the block before he could think of something else.

As Zee walked across the upper-school campus, she felt like an alien who had just landed on an unfamiliar planet (in her gas-guzzling spaceship). Sure, the upper-school kids were different, but it never mattered before. After all, they were the Others. Only, now she was one of them.

Don't Miss Any of
Mackenzie's
Middle School Adventures!
Mackenzie Blue
TINA WELLS
Mackenzie Blue
The Secret Crush
TINA WELLS
Mackenzie Blue
Friends Forever?
TINA WELLS
Mackenzie Blue
Mixed Messages
TINA WELLS
Available wherever books are sold.
www.harpercollinschildrens.com
HARPER
An Imprint of HarperCollinsPublishers